"I DON'T LIKE BEING INTERROGATED, GEORGIA,"

Wes warned. "But since we're going to be married in a few days, you've got a right to ask a few questions. Just remember, don't believe everything you hear. The reports of the women in my life have been greatly exaggerated."

He walked toward her slowly, his eyes never leaving her face.

"Which one do you want to know about?" he asked. "The first one?" He shrugged in indifference. "Sorry. I don't remember her name. The last one? That's easy. Her name's Georgia Dupree, soon to be Georgia Hayden. She's beautiful, pregnant, and she thinks too much. And no other woman has been able to make me forget her."

His hands settled on her shoulders. "Anything else?" he asked softly.

LINDA TURNER
A Glimpse of Heaven

Silhouette Desire

Originally Published by Silhouette Books
division of
Harlequin Enterprises Ltd.

First published in Great Britain 1985 by Silhouette Books, 15–16 Brook's Mews, London W1A 1DR

© Linda Turner 1985

Silhouette, Silhouette Desire and Colophon are Trade Marks of Harlequin Enterprises B.V.

ISBN 0 373 05220 0

225–1185

Printed and bound in Great Britain by Cox & Wyman Ltd, Reading

LINDA TURNER

is not only a writer but also a partner of a publishing company. She enjoys romance writing because it gives her a chance to travel extensively. She lives in Texas, and hopes to sail someday from her home to Maine.

1

The haunting notes of a trumpet drifted lazily on the evening air, the sensuous music winding through the narrow streets, enticing tourists to the garish bars of Bourbon Street. Twilight still lingered, but crowds were already beginning to gather. Before too long the air would throb with the potent combination of liquor, jazz, and the press of human bodies.

For a fleeting moment, Georgia Dupree watched the migration toward the nightlife of Bourbon Street from the steps of an old house on Bienville Street, but a singleness of purpose drew her green eyes back to the wooden door before her. Impatiently, she knocked again. Why didn't he answer the damn door?

She shifted her weight and glared at the tarnished brass knocker. Of course Wesley Hayden would have tarnished brass, she thought irritably. All the polish was applied to his own charming manners. He had slipped under her guard with a clownish grin, and she hadn't even noticed until it was too late. By then the damage had been done.

What a fool she'd been. She should have seen through that guileless grin and recognized him for the bewitching wolf he was. After all, David had warned her before Wes ever made the first trip to Baton Rouge to visit him. David Lee, assistant to the state attorney general, her boss and friend, had cautioned her not to be taken in by his old friend's boyish manner. Wesley Hayden's reputation was well known throughout the state. As the owner of Sam's Place, one of New Orleans' most popular restaurants and nightclubs, he was literally swamped with women, and he enjoyed every minute of it.

But she had ignored the warnings. Georgia had been so damned sure she could handle the man. She'd been exposed to his brand of charm all her life; she should have been immune to it. Her father was a master of the quick smile and innocuous flirtation that drew women to his side despite the presence of his wife. Her childhood had been spent watching her mother pretend she didn't care. She had vowed long ago that she wouldn't follow in her mother's footsteps. She loved her father, but she would never let herself fall in love with anyone like him.

No, she had been cocky, fully in control of her emotions and ready to put the oh so suave Mr. Hayden firmly in his place. But she hadn't been prepared for the laughter in his eyes. When he waltzed into her office in search of David and sat on the corner of her desk, flirting with her outrageously, she had been bewitched by the self-deprecating humor he didn't try to hide as he handed her one old line after another.

His laughter warmed her, and the ever present twinkle in his eyes disarmed her, until she began to wonder why she continued to fight against the attraction that had pulled at her from their first meeting. For one crazy month he had pursued her, burning up the miles between New Orleans and Baton Rouge every weekend. Despite her best intentions, despite her resolve to protect her precious independence, her body finally proved traitor to her mind. Wesley's hot passion melted her innate reserve and left her afire in his arms. When sanity returned with the morning sun, however, she knew she was dangerously close to repeating her mother's mistakes. It would be so easy to put herself into his hands, leaving her soul at his mercy.

She'd ended it then and there. Or so she had thought.

She lifted her clenched fist to the door, but it was jerked open before she touched it, leaving her hand in midair. She stiffened. The man she had dreamed about and cursed stood before her.

If she had secretly been hoping for a sign of joy, or at the very least surprise, she was disappointed. Cold and remote, Wesley's gaze revealed the tough, hard side of him, the side that had survived a childhood in New Orleans' slums. Georgia's heart jerked at the sight of him. He was dressed in evening clothes, the blackness of the suit coat dull compared to the midnight sheen of his hair. The classical lines of his clothes hugged his broad shoulders and lean hips, and he looked as if he didn't know the meaning of the word work. From the tips of his long, slender fingers to his well-shod feet he was the picture of elegance and sophistication. But she knew from experience that the front he presented to the world was deceptive. Beneath the clothes was a body that was hard, wiry, and strong. Several inches short of six feet, his streetwise machismo was well hidden. Wesley Hayden was a man used to fighting for what he wanted, and the tougher the opposition, the harder he fought. And he didn't always fight fair, Georgia reminded herself fiercely. She met his gaze unflinchingly. "May I come in?"

He lifted a dark brow arrogantly, but made no move to step out of the doorway. For a brief moment she panicked, afraid he might refuse. His stony gaze traveled over her with a remoteness that was chilling, and she was suddenly glad she had worn the tailored navy suit she usually wore in court. There would be no misunderstandings—this was strictly a business meeting. Mockery sprang into his eyes and pulled his sensuous mouth into a taunting smile, but he motioned her in. "Don't worry. I'm not going to slam the door in your face. Come in."

His invitation just bordered on curtness, but she hadn't really expected anything less from him. She had, after all, practically thrown him out of her apartment the last time she had seen him. "We have to talk, Wes. I—" She stopped short and felt her heart skid to a halt before jerkily resuming its rhythm.

Another woman. She stood framed in the wide double doors that opened off the entrance hall. Georgia's spirits sank as she noted the woman's dark auburn hair, intelligent sapphire eyes, and wide mouth. Why had she never considered the possibility that he might have found someone else? She couldn't expect him to remain faithful to an affair that was yesterday's news. Why not? her heart cried. She had. How had her mother stood all those years of watching her father with other women? How did she stand the pain?

Wes watched the determination fall from Georgia's face as she spied Jenny in the doorway and felt an angry satisfaction. What the hell had she expected? To turn up on his doorstep and be met by welcoming arms? Like hell! Every time he thought of that morning, when she had kicked him out of her bed and her life, he wanted to strangle her. "Why are you here, Georgia?" he demanded. "Have you decided to accept my offer?"

She glared at him, all the resentment and despair of the past few weeks bursting through her carefully constructed control. The suitcase she was clutching so desperately dropped to the floor with a loud bang. Her eyes never left his. "I'm pregnant," she said flatly.

She hadn't meant to tell him like this, to just blurt it out, and in front of a stranger, too. But he had goaded her. He was always goading her, damn him!

Pregnant! Wes took the announcement like a blow to the stomach. His breath left his lungs in a rush, leaving him stunned. Georgia was pregnant. With his child. He shook his head, trying to clear it. Surprise, doubt, joy bombarded him, only to be pushed aside by the memory of the last time they had seen each other. His eyes narrowed, sharpened into lances by the slow, burning anger in his gut. Jackass! he berated himself. What a clever trap she had laid, pretending that she wanted nothing from him when all the while she had been planning this. He'd been caught by the oldest trick in the book, all because of a pair of cool green eyes and a bewitching smile.

The woman at Wesley's side stirred uncomfortably. "I think I'd better leave," she said hurriedly, shooting a glance at Georgia before moving around her to the door. "I'll talk to you tomorrow, Wes."

"Fine. And thanks, Jenny." His eyes, however, were on Georgia. When the closing door signaled that they were alone he moved abruptly into the living room. "I need a drink." He glanced over his shoulder. "Want one? Or do pregnant women drink? I haven't had much experience."

Georgia's nails bit into her palms. He wasn't going to make this easy. "No, I don't want a drink. And I haven't had much experience either," she reminded him tersely as she stepped into the living room. "This is my first, remember?"

She watched him pour whiskey into a tumbler and felt her heart clench at the tight line of his jaw. His reaction was everything she had feared. A baby hardly fit into his life-style. He had built his own little empire from scratch; he answered to no one. And although he had many friends, he never permitted anyone to become too close, too important to him. Even when they had made love she had felt that there was a part of him always held in reserve. Nothing would ever be allowed to touch the essential core of him. Not even the baby.

Why did she care? She knew the pain of loving someone with his brand of charm, and she wouldn't love Wesley Hayden. She didn't want a man tying her down, limiting her career because his was more important. For years she had avoided emotional entanglements, devoting her passion to her education and the law. And it had paid off. She was a damn good lawyer; she didn't stand in the shadows and wait for men to remember her existence. She would never do that.

Wes slammed his glass down on the bar after draining the contents in one quick gulp. He suddenly looked every one of his thirty-three years. "Are you sure?"

She blinked in confusion at his hoarse question. "Sure? That I'm pregnant? Of course I'm . . ."

"Is the baby mine?" he interrupted in a hard voice. His grim gaze swept over her, lingering on her still slim waist before returning to her face. "I haven't seen you in two months. You could have been with someone else."

She gasped. "Yes! The baby is yours. Damn you, Wesley Hayden! Do you honestly think I'd foist someone else's child on you? Do you hate me that much?"

His eyes flared with an emotion she didn't understand. "No, I don't hate you. But you must admit I have reason to ask. We only made love once."

"That's all it takes!"

They glared at each other across a chasm of hostility. Seconds stretched into an eternity, but Georgia refused to be the first to lower her gaze. She couldn't afford to give him the slightest advantage. Determinedly, she lifted her chin and strengthened her nerve, but her knees were quivering when he finally expelled a heavy sigh. "This isn't getting us anywhere." He motioned to one of the blue camelback sofas flanking the fireplace. "Sit down and let's try to keep this civilized. Do you want money for an abortion?"

"No! I won't have an abortion, Wes. I mean it," she

said quietly as she sat down on the edge of the sofa. "Don't waste your breath trying to change my mind."

She hadn't thought it possible, but his expression became even grimmer. "Did I say I wanted you to have an abortion?" he demanded coldly. "You've obviously decided what you're going to do. Why don't you cut through this nonsense and tell me where I come into your plans."

"I'm going to keep the baby," she said simply, but her nails bit into her palms with the effort to maintain control of her emotions. She would not break down in front of him. "Don't worry, I don't want anything from you. But if you want to support your baby . . ."

"No."

"No?" she repeated stupidly, unable to drag her eyes from the harshness of his face. Her heart seemed to shatter at his words. How could he deny his own child? "If that's the way you want it," she said huskily. "But it is your baby, Wes."

"I know that," he replied calmly. "But I'm not going to pay for an illegitimate child."

"Who asked you to? I don't need you to support me or my baby. So you can relax, Wes. You're off scot-free. You can go your way, and the baby and I will go ours. We'll never have to cross each other's paths again."

"Don't threaten me, Georgia," he said softly. "I didn't say I wouldn't support my child. I won't support an illegitimate child."

She paled. "What are you saying?"

"We're going to get married." He rose and started walking toward her.

"No! Is that why you think I'm here? To force a

proposal out of you?'' She laughed shortly, without humor, her eyes stinging with the irony of the situation. Marriage was the last thing she wanted. "This changes nothing, Wes. Two months ago I refused to live with you. What makes you think I'd marry you just because I'm pregnant?''

"Because I won't have a bastard child!" he ground out fiercely. For the first time his face registered the emotions he usually kept hidden. Resentment, fury, hurt—it was all there in the haggard lines of his face and the clouded depths of his eyes. His slender fingers reached out to grab her shoulders, biting into her skin with barely controlled anger. Georgia stood within his grasp, unable to protest, unable to do anything but stare at a side of Wesley Hayden she had never seen before.

"No child of mine will go through what I went through.'' A spasm of pain drew furrowed lines across his forehead, the sudden ringing of childish taunts sounded in his ears; childhood memories, uncertainties, guilt flickered before his eyes. He tried to shake them off, but failed. "My son won't grow up wondering who his old man is or what his name really is. He's a Hayden and that sure as hell is the name he's going to have. Do I make myself clear, Georgia? I won't let you do to my son what my mother did to me. If you didn't want to marry me, you shouldn't have gotten pregnant.''

"I didn't do it on purpose,'' she cried. "Do you think I planned this?''

He had to give her credit, he thought bitterly. She was playing the part right up to the end, and she was one hell of an actress. If he didn't know better, he'd have sworn she was terrified of marriage. He wanted to grab her and shake the truth out of her, but if he ever touched her, he might not let her go.

The implacable, unrevealing lines of his face were closed to her, but she was too caught up in her reeling thoughts to notice that he hadn't answered her question. A bastard. She hadn't known. Wes never talked about his family, his childhood. And she had never even suspected the bitterness he harbored. Was that the secret he hid behind his usual laughing unconcern? How could she fight the memories of his childhood and ignore his plea? He would hate her if she refused him, and she didn't think she could live with that. But how could she accept? "I don't want to get married. And neither do you. Why does a baby have to change things?"

"Don't be obtuse," he snapped. "You're carrying my son or daughter. If you've really got a hang-up about making a commitment, you'll just have to get over it. I'm not going to let that affect the future happiness of my child. We're going to be married just as soon as I can arrange it."

"I don't have a hang-up about making a commitment! Quit twisting everything I say!"

Agitation carried her to her feet. "I'm not here to discuss the past." She stepped closer to him, her eyes accusing as they met his. "You made it perfectly clear what you wanted in a relationship, and I can see you haven't changed. I'm expected to give up my career and my life in Baton Rouge just to accommodate you. Thanks, but no thanks. That's not what I call a commitment."

"Don't you think you're being a little ridiculous?" The muscles along his jaw rippled in growing anger.

"My business is here in New Orleans. I can't pack it up and move to Baton Rouge just because you don't want to move here. Anyway, that's ancient history. The circumstances have changed. You're going to marry me."

"No, I'm not!"

"Do you care so little for your own child?"

"No, I . . ." Furious, she blinked back tears, confused by her emotions. Why was she so hurt that he hadn't uttered one endearment or made a move to touch her with anything but anger? She had destroyed any feelings he had for her when she hustled him out of her apartment and shut him out of her life. "What about my career?" she asked huskily. "I've worked hard to get where I am. I don't want to give it up."

"You'll eventually have to take maternity leave anyway," he reasoned, watching her carefully. What had brought the shadows to her eyes? There were moments when a sadness he couldn't fathom gripped her. She had given herself to him completely, yet she still held him at arm's length. "After the baby is born you can go back to work if you want to."

She sighed. "Wes, don't you realize it would never work? We'd be marrying for all the wrong reasons. What kind of life would that be for the baby, brought into a home where its parents don't even love each other? We'd all be miserable."

"Not necessarily. We weren't miserable when I was seeing you every weekend, were we?"

"But it didn't last. Physical attraction isn't enough. Anyway, I don't want to get married." He would never change—he would always attract women without half trying, and she didn't want to share the man she gave her heart to with every woman who walked into his restaurant.

He stiffened at her words. "Join the club. In case you hadn't noticed, I'm not exactly thrilled either. But my child is going to have a name and a father. After he's born I won't stand in your way if you want a divorce."

"And what about custody?" she demanded, trying to ignore the voice screaming in her head. How could she even think of marrying a man who was already discussing divorce? "If you're going to fight for custody, I won't marry you."

His opaque eyes flashed with a hint of steel. "If the issue comes up, we'll discuss it then."

"*When* the issue comes up we won't have to discuss it," she countered firmly. "I won't even consider marrying you without a prenuptial agreement."

For the first time he grinned. "Are you afraid I'm after your money?"

Her heart turned over and she fought the emotion the only way she knew how—with anger. "No. I haven't got enough to argue over. And I'm certainly not after yours. I'm just protecting my baby. You'll have to agree *in writing* that you won't fight for custody."

His humor vanished as quickly as it had appeared, leaving behind a self-deprecating smile. "I should have known better than to get mixed up with a lady lawyer. Can I trust you to be fair?"

"If you can't, we shouldn't even be discussing marriage," she retorted dryly. "But just to make sure, you'd better have your lawyer check it out. *If* I decide to marry you."

"You will," he replied confidently. "You can't fool

me. You care more about this baby than you're letting on. You won't do anything to hurt your own child."

The truth of his words echoed in Georgia's heart like the slamming of a jail-cell door. He was right, of course. As soon as she had heard the results of the pregnancy test, she had known she would do anything for her baby. She hadn't expected Wes to push for marriage, though. For twenty-nine years she had avoided that particular commitment. Just the thought of giving herself to a man who was so much like her father scared the hell out of her. She had to get out of here and give herself time to think. She grabbed her purse. "That's why I'm making sure now that there won't be a custody fight later. If that's all we have to discuss . . ."

He stepped in front of her, cutting off her escape. "And just where do you think you're going?"

"H–home, of course," she stuttered around the sudden lump in her throat. "I packed a bag in case I had to stay the weekend. That's not necessary now that we've had a chance to talk." She made a move to step around him, careful not to touch him. "Let me know what you decide about the prenuptial agreement and—"

"I'll sign it," he growled softly and stopped her efforts to escape with the simple touch of his finger on her chin. His eyes met hers. "You can stay here tonight. I don't like the idea of my future wife and unborn child alone on the highway after dark."

The warmth of his touch on her skin set all her nerve endings clamoring, and she closed her eyes weakly as memories washed over her. What was she getting herself into? They weren't even married yet, and he was already giving her orders and trying to take charge of her life. "Wes . . ."

"When are you going to marry me?"

Her eyes flew open. "I haven't said I will. You have to give me time to think. We wouldn't be in this mess now if you had given me time to think."

"Some things don't have to be thought about." His fingers moved to the curve of her cheek. "Quit analyzing everything and go with your instincts. I promise you you won't make the wrong decision."

The husky depth of his voice slid down her spine, caressing her, stirring to life old flames she had tried desperately to extinguish. He could seduce her with a word, a look. For a timeless moment she stood captured by his magnetism, surrounded by memories and the unexpected reality of his masculinity.

But he'll hurt you, the voice cried. *He doesn't love you. He's only marrying you because of the baby.*

No! her heart cried, but it was too late. The truth stared her boldly in the face, and she had no choice but to accept it.

"If I had followed my instincts," she said in a low voice, "I never would have come here tonight. I would have had the baby and you would have been none the wiser. But the baby is yours, and I wanted you to know you're going to be a father."

The timbre of her voice urged him to wrap his arms around her even though he knew that was the last thing she wanted from him. She wouldn't let him hold her, at least not now. So he reached for her suitcase instead and lifted it effortlessly. Three steps up the stairs, he turned to grin at her, his dark eyes twinkling devilishly. "You can sleep in my room. I want you within reach."

"Wes!" she protested sharply, fighting the pull his smile had on her heartstrings. "You're not going to rush me into anything. I told you I need some time."

"I'd be glad to give it to you, sweetheart, but we haven't got it. I'll see about making the arrangements tomorrow."

"I won't sleep with you," she called up the stairs to him. "So if you think you can seduce me into changing my mind, you're wasting your time."

From the top of the stairs he turned and looked down at her. There was an air of determination about him that would not be denied. "You *will* sleep with me," he countered softly. "I told you, I intend to keep you close. But don't worry. I won't touch you unless you ask me to."

She gasped. Of all the arrogant nerve! "Then we have nothing to worry about, do we? I'll never ask."

"Don't be too sure of that," he warned with a grin. "The baby won't be here for almost seven months. A lot can happen between now and then. Who knows? You might even fall in love with me."

2

∾∞∞∞∞∞∞∞∞∞

The sunlight that spilled cheerfully into the room hours later was met by a groan. The bed was just as empty as when Georgia had climbed into it. How many times had she reached for him in the night only to have her searching fingers encounter nothing but thin air? She had waited up until three A.M., caught up in the masculine scent of him that clung to the sheets, caught up in breathless memories.

She was a first-class idiot. Wes had threatened the convictions of a lifetime with his insistence on marriage, and what had she done? Meekly gone along with him. Tiredness and tension must have loosened a screw in her brain; there was no other explanation. The hope that he felt more than physical attraction for her had taken a stranglehold on her reason, but now she could see things clearly. He might have offered marriage, but that was only for the sake of the baby. He had no intention of making a commitment.

Anger sparkled in her eyes, lighting the fuse on her resentment. This was all wrong. She was in his home—his bed, no less—surrounded by his most prized possessions, and where was he? Out on the prowl like an alley cat who didn't know when to call it a night!

Marriage to him would be impossible.

That thought blinked in her mind like a neon sign, illuminating the secret recesses of her heart, where hope foolishly lingered. Ruthlessly, she destroyed the dreams, the fantasies, and faced cold reality. She had done her duty by telling Wes he would soon be a father. Nothing else was required of her, certainly not marriage to a man whose path was so divergent from her own. She could go back to Baton Rouge with a clear conscience and try to forget that Wesley Hayden had ever turned her life upside-down.

With more haste than grace, she threw off her light cotton nightgown and jerked on jeans and a sleeveless yellow blouse. Critically, she surveyed her figure in the mirror, her hand automatically sliding to her stomach, as it had countless times during the last few weeks. A baby. The knowledge that she was pregnant continued to amaze her. Twenty-nine-year-old career women didn't make this kind of mistake, and she had to admit she'd been furious when she first heard the news. It changed everything—her carefully made plans, her body, her life. But it would be for the better, she told herself determinedly as she pulled her shoulder-length blond hair into a ponytail. Her baby would have the best life she could give it, and there would be no regrets.

Downstairs, she set her suitcase by the front door before going in search of the kitchen. For the first time in weeks she was starving, and not even the threat of Wes's return could stop her from eating. But the beauty of the old house caught her unaware. Her feet dragged, and for the first time since her arrival she really looked at her surroundings. Located in the Vieux Carré, the original Franco-Spanish city of the Creoles, the house had been built around a courtyard that offered its inhabitants complete privacy. Wide French doors in the living room opened to a garden overflowing with greenery. Magnolia and banana trees as well as gardenias, cannas, and geraniums provided a colorful retreat from the humidity that seemed to rise with the temperature. Georgia wanted to explore the hidden recesses of the garden and house, but the little voice that reminded her she couldn't stay wouldn't allow her the luxury. As soon as she ate breakfast, she was leaving.

But at the sight of the kitchen she was lost. Compared to the rest of the house it was small, but every inch of space was utilized. The stove and a butcher-block counter created an island work area around which cabinets lined three walls, providing plenty of storage space. Directly over the work area hung a selection of pots, pans, and utensils that would make a chef's mouth water. And, as in the living room, French doors offered access to the patio. Positioned in front of the doors was a round, glass-topped rattan table with four matching throne chairs.

She'd never dreamed Wes would have a kitchen like this. It was straight out of *Better Homes and Gardens,* and she loved it.

The refrigerator, however, only held a couple of cans of beer, a few eggs, and a blackened banana. Didn't he know better than to put a banana in the refrigerator? she wondered as she picked it up and tossed it in the trash. So much for appearances. He probably hadn't eaten at home in months, but then, why should he when he owned his own restaurant?

She melted butter in a small skillet and had just cracked an egg into it when an overwhelming wave of nausea hit her. A cold sweat suddenly drenched her body, and the hand she raised to her throat was anything but steady. "Oh no!" she moaned. She couldn't be sick, not now. But her mind couldn't reason with her heaving stomach, and with jerky movements she turned off the burner under the skillet and made a mad dash for the bathroom.

In the hallway she ran full tilt into a masculine chest. Her eyes flew up to the face above her. "Wes . . . where . . ."

Her paleness, the trembling hand at her throat told him everything he needed to know. He pushed open the door at his shoulder and pulled her in after him. "In here." His eyes darkened with concern. "Are you all right?"

She groaned as another wave of nausea threatened her control. Why did he have to see her like this? Surely he'd rather be a million miles away. "Please," she choked. "Go away!"

He ignored her, the rock-hard support of his arms sliding around the back of her waist while his other hand held her head. "It's okay, baby. You'll feel better in a minute," he soothed gruffly. "Just lean on me."

She didn't want to lean on him, but she couldn't seem to stop herself. Mortification curled her toes. She'd never feel better again, and it was all his fault. Why didn't he just go away and leave her alone? she wondered bitterly as she was finally able to sink to the side of the tub. Weak and spent, she could only summon a halfhearted protest when he wet a washcloth and began to wash her face. "Wes, please, I'm not a child."

"Quit trying to be so damn independent. Let someone take care of you for once in your life." Annoyed with himself for growling at her, he cursed softly under his breath. She was just as prickly now as she'd been the first day he'd seen her. Prim and proper in a conservative suit, with her hair scraped back from her face and frost in her eyes, she had looked down that pert nose of hers and dismissed him before he'd even had a chance to open his mouth. He had wanted her from that very moment, but it had taken him weeks to get past the icy barriers she'd constructed to the warm, passionate woman within.

He tilted up her chin and continued his ministrations, a frown darkening his brow. She was too damn pale, and he didn't like the clouds in her eyes. Regardless of whether or not she had deliberately gotten pregnant, she was obviously worrying herself sick over it, and his picking at her wouldn't help her present condition. He could sense the fear in her, the hurt, though the cause was a mystery to him. And if he tried to probe, she'd probably snap his head off. Now wasn't the time to break down her defenses, though he'd have liked nothing better than to hold her in his arms again. Instead, he pushed back the strands of golden hair that had escaped her ponytail and relaxed as the color gradually came back into her face. "Feeling better?"

She nodded, too mesmerized by the gentleness in his eyes to speak. When he ranted and raved at her she could stand toe to toe with him and fend off his angry words with a few of her own. But his tenderness completely destroyed her.

"Good." He swept her up into his arms, a huge grin splitting his face. "But in your delicate condition you shouldn't overdo. We're going to have to do something about fattening you up."

"I'm not a cow going to slaughter," she reminded him tightly, studiously trying to ignore the sudden trip-hammer beat of her heart. "And I'm perfectly capable of walking. Put me down."

He chuckled, delighted by her outrage. Now she had some life in her! Purposefully, he strode into the living room, cradling her close. Damn, but she felt right in his arms! This was a side of marriage he was definitely going to enjoy.

"I told you to put me down, Wes."

A dark brow lifted over suddenly dancing eyes. "Do you always get your way with men?"

"Yes!"

"Not this man." Without warning, Georgia found herself on the couch, firmly settled on his lap. At her furious gasp, he laughed. "When are you going to learn you can't order me about like other men? The icy Miss Dupree doesn't scare me in the least. You should know that by now." With a soft touch he smoothed the frown from her brow before trailing his finger down her cheek to trace the outline of her stubbornly set mouth. His hungry gaze snared hers. "I've tasted the fire in you, honey. I won't let you hide behind the ice."

How could he accuse her of being icy, she thought wildly, her lips throbbing from his caress. Couldn't he feel the heat in her? With the simple touch of his fingers he had her burning for his touch, his taste. The

27

velvet sheathed by his unyielding, steely exterior caught her on the blind side, and without even realizing how it had happened, he had totally undermined her defenses. Even when she knew he had been out all night . . .

She stiffened. The long lonely hours she had waited for the sound of his footsteps on the stairs came flooding back to boil her blood. Her eyes sparkled dangerously. Damn him! How dare he come home as if nothing had happened? Why, he still had on his evening clothes! She pulled away from his touch and sat stiffly on his lap, her arms hugging her chest. "Is that what you were doing last night?" she asked coldly. "Tasting the fire in someone else?"

One dark brow lifted over glittering eyes that trapped her on his lap. "Is that what you think I was doing?"

His low growl slid down her spine like an ice cube, and too late Georgia realized she might have pushed him too far. "Wes . . . I didn't mean—"

"Answer me, damn it!" he snarled. "You're the one who started this. Don't stop now. Where do you think I was?"

"I haven't the foggiest," she snapped. She'd be damned if she'd apologize for her suspicions. She had a right to every one of them. Hadn't she walked in last night and found him with another woman? What was she supposed to think when he disappeared until breakfast? "If you weren't with another woman, then where were you? I know you spend a lot of time at the restaurant, but even you wouldn't stay there all night."

"That's exactly where I was."

The quiet admission stabbed her reproachfully. Her eyes flew to his. "But why?"

Mockery pulled his lips into a crooked grin. "Would you believe I was trying to be thoughtful? I thought you might need some time to yourself, so I slept on the couch in my office. But if I'd known you were going to get this upset, I'd have come home. From now on I'll be here."

The promise in his words had her tearing his hands from her waist in panic. The trap was closing. "Don't come home on my account. I won't be here. Let go! I'm going home."

His hands clamped around her like a hawk snaring its prey. "Be still," he ordered roughly. "You're not going anywhere until we get this straightened out." She had to be the most stubborn woman he had ever met! She was fighting him every inch of the way, but he couldn't help remembering a time when anger had been the last thing she'd felt for him. He wanted that warm, willing woman in his arms again, and he was going to have her! "Do you honestly think I would propose to you and then spend the night with another woman?" he demanded softly.

"I don't know what to think," she cried. "We may have made a baby together, but you're still a stranger. I can no more predict what you would do than I can a man on the street." A shuddering breath tore through her, and her shoulders drooped in defeat. "Let me go, Wes. I want to go home."

He shook his head. "I'd just come after you. Would you please explain to me what happened between last night and this morning to change your mind about us getting married? I've explained where I was, so it can't be that. Come on, Georgia, tell me. I can't read your mind."

"Let's just say I finally came to my senses," she replied coolly. "I had a lot of time to think, and this morning I decided to . . ."

"You weren't thinking, you were panicking," he interrupted, devilish lights of laughter sneaking into his eyes. "Haven't you realized yet that you aren't a morning person, sweetheart? You should never do any serious thinking until after you've had your first cup of coffee." When she only glared at him his grin broadened. "I realized that the morning after we made love. All night long you couldn't keep your hands off me, but when I kissed you awake you knocked me out of the bed! I knew then I was in for trouble."

"Don't you dare lay all the blame on me," she objected indignantly, the warmth generated by his teasing fading in the face of an icy memory. That had been one of the worst days of her life, and she'd never be able to laugh about it. "You weren't in a cheerful mood yourself. In fact, you were furious when I didn't jump at the chance to move in with you. Well, pardon me for bruising your fragile male ego. I didn't realize your proposition was a compliment."

Her sarcasm tightened his mouth into a grim line. "Believe me, it was. I wouldn't ask just any woman to live with me, though there are some who *would* jump at the chance."

"Then go ask them," she choked, her voice thickening with pain. "Just make sure there are no misunderstandings. Then you won't have to accuse some poor, unsuspecting girl of using her body to wring a proposal out of you. I believe you called it 'sexual blackmail,'" she reminded him.

The hurt in her voice went straight to his heart. He

couldn't question her distress, but was it fear that he would see through her ruse that hurt her more than his words? He'd already played a gullible fool once; it wasn't a role he cared to repeat. "Were you trying to force a proposal out of me?"

"No! How many times do I have to say it? I don't want to get married. To you or anyone else. It would never work."

"Don't you think you should give it a chance first?" he asked dryly. "I never would have thought you were a quitter, but you're giving up without even a fight. What's the matter? Don't you think you can hack it?"

"No. I mean yes!" she cried, his goading voicing her own doubts. She hit him in the chest with a clenched fist. "Damn it, Wes, I won't let you do this! I know what you're doing and it won't work."

He grabbed her hand and kissed the white knuckles before bringing it down and holding it against his chest. At her silent, determined struggle for freedom, he grinned. "What am I doing?"

"You're throwing down the gauntlet, but I'm not going to pick it up. You won't dare me into marriage."

"Foiled again," he said, his soft laughter embracing her.

"That's right." At last the anger was gone. She met his gaze earnestly, trying to ignore his nearness, the strength of his body beneath her, the memory of his hair-roughened legs entwined with hers. "You're thirty-three years old," she said hoarsely. "You've never answered to anyone in your life and you're not going to start now. Last night proved that."

"Last night proved nothing," he objected, frowning, "except that you needed me to calm your doubts, and I misunderstood the signals you were sending out. I thought you needed space."

"We both need space, more than marriage will allow." At the sight of his black brows knit together and no sign of comprehension in the eyes watching her as if she were a new item on the menu, she sighed in exasperation. "Why are you being so stubborn? What's the point of tying us together when we're both going to continue to go our separate ways?"

"I'll tell you the point," he replied gruffly. His hand slid to her abdomen, protectively covering the fragile life that beat there and loosening her heart from its moorings. At the involuntary tightening of her stomach muscles, his eyes glowed with warmth. "Lady, that's one hell of an argument you're carrying around. Nothing you can say will change the fact that that baby needs two parents. And one thing you've got to admit is that our marriage will never be boring. We're very much alike. Independent, stubborn as hell, and determined to have our own way. We'll probably have some terrific fights. Which leads to my second point."

His mouth was suddenly just inches away from hers, his breath caressing her lips, her cheeks, warming her blood as his arms twined around her to draw her close. "Making up will be fantastic," he growled huskily. He hadn't meant to rush her, to force an intimacy she neither wanted nor was ready for. But she was too close, and her sweet body was giving off nothing but heat. He couldn't fight the urge to mold her to him and let his hands glory in the feel of her. God, she was soft. With infinite tenderness he took her mouth again and again in tempting kisses that teased and flirted with the fire in her. A quiver she couldn't suppress ran through her, and his body instantly responded. With a groan, he murmured against her mouth, "Georgia, sweetheart, open yourself to me. You know you want to. Don't fight me."

She wasn't fighting him; she was battling the urge to forget her objections to what was surely madness, to forget the world and let him take her to their own special universe where nothing and no one could intrude. Her heart coaxed her to melt with the sweet flow of longing that coursed through her like honey and turned her bones to water. A white, hot flame sparked in the center of her being, flaring brighter with each touch of his hands, each kiss, threatening the barriers that protected her too vulnerable heart. The need to touch him, to feel his desire, to experience again his total possession became a physical ache that tore at her self-control. But reason screamed in protest, reasserting itself. With a moan, she pulled free of his mouth and buried her face against his chest, the pounding of his heartbeat echoing in her ear. His warmth surrounded her, and she couldn't keep her arms from holding him tight.

"Please, Wes, don't!" she cried into his shirtfront. "I can't get involved with you again."

He could feel the battle being waged within her and wondered if it could be anything like what he himself was experiencing. With a few more kisses he could probably win both the wars, but she'd only end up resenting him more. Grimly, he stared down at her bent head. "I hate to disillusion you, but we're already involved. I can't let you hide your head in the sand and pretend we're not. I know I'm not the world's greatest catch, but I didn't think you'd be that opposed to marrying me."

Was that hurt she heard in his voice? She pulled back to look into his eyes, and the vulnerability she saw there completely undermined her resolve. She felt herself weaken. How could she explain to him the confusion of her own emotions? "There're so many things you don't understand. . . ."

"So explain them to me."

The words that hovered on her tongue finally spilled forth. "Who's Jenny? And why did you have to go to the restaurant last night? I know you said you had a problem, but I'll bet you twenty dollars it's a problem that wears skirts. Don't you see? I know all about your reputation, and I'm not going to marry a man who has more women than he knows what to do with. I can't help the way I feel. . . ."

"Whoa, whoa!" Wes laughed, delight sparkling in his eyes, a huge grin softening the stern angles of his face. "You're jealous!"

"No, I'm not."

"Yes, you are," he chuckled, "and there's no need." He reached up to massage the tense muscles of her neck, unable to wipe the amusement from his face. "Sweetheart, you're jumping to all the wrong conclusions. Jenny is a neighbor, and a good friend. I should have introduced you last night, but at the time I wasn't in the mood to offer any explanations. As for the problem at work, one of my employees was having a problem with her son. She wanted me to have a talk with him."

"Are you trying to tell me you haven't been seeing anyone since we split up?"

Wariness crept into his eyes. "I'm not a monk, Georgia."

"My point exactly." She scrambled off his lap and

escaped to the doors opening onto the patio before turning to glare at him. "You want me to marry you at least until the baby is born, but how many women am I going to trip over in the meantime? It's not a question of jealousy. I don't want to get lost in the crowd."

"Damn it, there haven't been that many!" he bellowed. He stalked toward her. "I don't like being interrogated, but since we're going to be married in a few days, you've got a right to ask a few questions. Just remember, don't believe everything you hear. The reports on the women in my life have been greatly exaggerated. Which ones do you want to know about? The first one?" He shrugged in indifference. "Sorry. I don't remember her name. The last one? That's easy. Her name's Georgia Dupree, soon to be Georgia Hayden. She's beautiful, pregnant, and she thinks too much. And no other woman has been able to make me forget her. Anything else you want to know?"

His hands settled on her shoulders, the pounding of her heart tripling with his admission. She was suddenly breathless. "Are you in love with this woman you're planning on marrying?"

He hesitated, turning her heart to stone. His hands fell away from her, his eyes suddenly bottomless. "I don't know," he finally admitted. "I probably wouldn't know love if it hit me in the face. I'm not even sure it exists."

Shock widened her eyes, and without thinking, she blurted out, "How can you say that? Of course it exists! Your mother must have—"

"My mother neither knew nor cared where I was most of the time," he lashed out. "She worked nights in a dive on Bourbon Street and slept days. We saw as little as possible of each other."

The cold hardness of his face chilled her. "Wes . . . I'm sorry," she floundered. "I didn't know. . . ."

He shrugged. "It's not important. I only told you so you won't hold out for my love. You'd only be disappointed."

The shutters were back in place; he wasn't going to allow her to get any closer. She knew she should have been devastated. The father of her child was refusing to love her. But the lonely little boy he had allowed her to glimpse briefly was crying out to her, and it was a plea she couldn't ignore. There was hope for them yet, regardless of the way Wes claimed he felt now. She wasn't giving up on the man she was close to losing her heart to.

3

‑∞∞∞∞∞∞∞∞∞∞‑

I still don't see what the all-fired hurry is," she said as they headed for Baton Rouge later that day. "The baby isn't due for months. We don't have to rush into anything."

Wes sighed impatiently. "We've been all through this, Georgia. There's no reason to postpone the inevitable."

"There's every reason," she insisted stubbornly. "I can't drop everything and move to New Orleans in a few hours. What about my apartment? My furniture?"

"I'll take care of it," he promised. "But the move's got to be now. It would be too hard on you when you're farther along in your pregnancy. And I can't spare the time later. I'm in the middle of expanding my restaurant. This is my only free weekend."

"Well, excuse me for getting in your way," she

snapped. "Why don't I take you back to New Orleans, and we'll forget the whole thing."

Wes heard the pain in her voice and cursed his own clumsiness. Damn it, he didn't want to hurt her, but he couldn't seem to stop himself. He straightened in his seat, annoyance flickering in his eyes. "I didn't mean it that way, and you know it. I'm just trying to make you see reason. . . ."

"Why don't you try logic then? All this rushing isn't necessary. I have too much to do. And I can't quit without giving David notice. He needs me. . . ."

"I need you more," Wes interrupted her gruffly. It wasn't an admission he made easily, but he ached with the need to hold her. If she wasn't driving, if they were anywhere but in the middle of the highway, he'd show her what real need was. "I can't let you stay in Baton Rouge. I intend to take care of you and the baby, and I can't do that long distance."

His husky voice slid over her, caressing her, stirring the embers of a desire that had never really died. Her widened eyes searched his face. Why did he want to take care of her? He didn't have to. She didn't want him to. Unless he loved her. Her eyes met his. "How do you think I got by without you for twenty-nine years?"

"Lord knows," he laughed. "It must have been damn difficult." At her unladylike snort, he reached over to squeeze her knee, his dark eyes alight with a lazy sensuality that stole her breath. Slowly, his fingers moved up her inner thigh, tracing the inside seam of her jeans. "One of these days," he growled, "you're going to admit you can't live without me."

Georgia gasped as desire flashed deep within her, stunning her. What this man could do to her with only the touch of his fingers was positively wicked. If she wasn't careful, she could become addicted to it. And that would be fatal when their marriage ended. She wouldn't walk away with a broken heart. She reached for his hand and deliberately pulled it from her leg. "Don't hold your breath," she advised coolly. "I'm not a romantic, Wes. I don't need a man to make me happy."

His eyes narrowed dangerously. What had he said to bring back the ice? He searched the delicate lines of her face, noting without surprise her closed expression, the wariness. What was she afraid of? Surely not him? He just wanted to hold her, to calm her fears. "You don't need to freeze me out," he told her softly. "I won't hurt you."

Hurt her? she thought wildly. He had the power to destroy her, and he didn't even know it. "I don't know what you're talking about," she denied stiffly.

"Oh, yes you do. You're afraid of me, and for the life of me, I can't figure out why. But I will," he promised, "I will."

She bit back a scathing retort and focused her attention on her driving. He was flattering himself if he thought she was afraid of him or any other man. He could only hurt her if she let him, and she had no intention of being that stupid.

The silence between them stretched into an eternity, and to her chagrin, Georgia discovered that ignoring Wesley Hayden was no easy task. Her body throbbed with the knowledge of his touch, refusing to forget the ecstasy he had taught her. How was she going to endure the next seven months without going out of her mind?

By the time they reached her apartment she was a

nervous wreck. She hurried inside, but Wes was only a step behind her, his warm breath caressing her hair, heating her blood. In desperation, she turned to him. "Don't you have something you can do while I start packing?"

Laughter danced in his eyes. "Not a thing. Why? Are you trying to get rid of me?"

"And if I am?"

"Too bad." He dropped to the couch, a delighted grin lighting his face. She wasn't as immune to his presence as she'd like to pretend. Maybe he was finally cracking that shell she'd built around herself. "I'm going to stick around to make sure you don't overdo it."

"Damn it, Wes, will you lay off! You've got to quit treating me like a porcelain doll. I'm as healthy as a horse, and all this pampering is driving me crazy!"

His good humor vanished, leaving his face grim, determined. "I do have a vested interest here, you know," he said harshly. "That's my baby you're carrying around, and I'm going to make damn sure nothing happens to it."

"You don't think I'd deliberately try to lose the baby, do you?" she choked.

"Don't be ridiculous," he snapped impatiently. "You could have had an abortion if you didn't want the baby." Thank God she hadn't! Lightning swift, he grabbed her wrist and pulled her onto his lap. At the sight of her mutinous face, a bittersweet smile played about the corners of his mouth. She was so damn stubborn that sometimes he just wanted to kiss her into submission. Did she have any idea what she did to him? He sighed. "I know this is difficult for you, honey. A husband and baby don't fit into your plans right now. But humor me. *Please.* Believe it or not, this baby means a lot to me, and I don't want to be left out. Let me take care of you and the baby and enjoy the waiting just like any other expectant father."

How could she refuse him when he looked at her with such longing? she wondered with a dry sob. He wasn't fighting fair, but she couldn't shut him out. Not when she remembered the loneliness of his childhood. Giving his hand a quick squeeze, she slipped from his arms, putting distance between them before she turned to confront him. "If you're going to stay, you might as well make yourself useful. You can see about having the furniture stored while I pack."

He nodded, accepting the unspoken truce she offered. "Anything else?"

"I've got six more months on my lease. Think you can get me out of it?"

"No problem." He watched her walk toward her bedroom, fighting the unexpected urge to follow her. "If you need any help," he called softly, "just whistle."

"I will," she promised. She went to the closet and pulled out her luggage. She had to keep busy, keep moving. It was the only way to blot out the past and avoid the future, the pain she knew was sure to come.

"How's it coming?" Wes asked as he stuck his head around the door an hour later. At the sight of her staggering under an armload of clothes from the closet, he frowned and crossed the room in three long strides. "What the hell do you think you're doing?" Angrily, he took the suits and dresses from her and dumped them on the bed. "Why didn't you ask for help?"

"Because I didn't need any." She straightened the

tumbled clothes before they wrinkled, her green eyes sparkling dangerously as they ran full tilt into his. "You're doing it again."

"What?"

"Treating me like a helpless female."

He frowned. "You're a far cry from helpless, Georgia."

"I know. I was beginning to wonder if you did."

His eyes locked with hers. "You know, there's such a thing as being too independent. Why don't you relax and enjoy being cherished? At least while you're pregnant."

His unknowing words touched off memories that had faded with time. The years slipped away, and Georgia saw her mother pregnant with her younger brother, her father's attentiveness before the baby was born, his wandering eye when things returned to normal. God, she didn't want that. "I can't," she whispered.

The sadness in her eyes struck him to the heart. Where had it come from? He reached for her. "Georgia, honey, what's wrong?"

"I . . . nothing." Determinedly, she shook off the threatening melancholy and pinned on a smile that wavered only slightly. "Did you make the arrangements to have everything stored?"

"The movers will be here next week. And the landlord agreed to release you from your lease."

Her brows shot up in surprise. "How did you manage that?"

Wicked mischief glittered in his eyes. "I told him we were running off to get married, and if he didn't release you from your lease, he'd be standing in the way of true love. His wife agreed."

"You didn't!"

"Yes, I did." He laughed. He stepped over to the dresser and idly toyed with her perfume, his eyes suddenly wary as they met hers in the mirror. "I also called your father," he said quietly. "We're having dinner with him and your brother."

She stiffened. "I thought we were going back to New Orleans tonight."

"We were. But this is the perfect opportunity for me to meet your family. We'll spend the night and go back in the morning."

Her eyes fell on her full-size bed—the only bed in the apartment—and her heart sank. How could she share that bed with him and her memories? She couldn't. She turned on him, her panic twisting into anger. "Don't you think we should have discussed this?"

Bewildered, Wes demanded, "What's there to discuss? Don't I have the right to meet my future father-in-law?"

"You don't have the right to interfere," she snapped. "My father knows nothing about you or the baby. I wanted to tell him when the time was right."

"Before or after we made him a grandfather? I didn't tell your father about us or the baby. I left that to you."

"That was decent of you, since you're the one who put me in this position. What am I going to tell him? That I'm pregnant? That you're only marrying me because you have to?"

"That's enough!" he snarled, snatching her into his arms before the taunting words were even out of her mouth. "If you're trying to start a fight, you're certainly going about it the right way."

Mortification sickened her. She was acting like a first-class fool. "Wes . . . I'm sorry. I don't know why I said those things."

"Maybe you're nervous about tonight?" he suggested quietly. The tension slowly drained out of him, but his eyes were watchful as they rested on her face. "It's perfectly understandable."

"Tonight?" she choked, her voice breaking as his hands began to absently explore her back. Lethargy weakened her limbs, coaxing her to forget her fears and put herself in his hands. She shifted her shoulders in a halfhearted attempt to escape. "Don't be ridiculous. I'm just tired. Now let me go. I've still got a lot to do."

"Not until you admit I'm right about tonight."

A slim brow arched delicately. "And why would I be nervous about having dinner with my father?"

"I don't know. Why don't you tell me?" At her stubborn silence, he laughed softly. "No go, huh? I guess I'll just have to find another way to convince you to talk."

In one swift motion, he captured her hands and planted a lingering kiss on the inside of each wrist before placing her arms around his neck. Fire leaped through Georgia's veins, the sudden pounding of her heart robbing her of breath. "Wes—"

"Ssh," he commanded huskily, his warm breath gently caressing her lips. He felt the struggle going on inside her, the wariness, the doubts, and logic warned him not to push her, to give her time. But how could he when she was so damn soft in his arms? He pulled her closer, the sweetness of her scent going straight to his head. "You had your chance to talk. Now it's my turn."

She saw the desire in his eyes and panicked. "No!" she choked, pushing at his shoulders. She couldn't give herself to him again. "Let me go, Wes."

"Not on your life," he growled, burying his head in the curve of her neck, his slender fingers tugging her hair free of its restricting band, loving the feel of its blond silkiness. He'd never let her go now that he had her back. He pressed a kiss to the corner of her mouth. "God, I've missed you, sweetheart," he rasped thickly. "The nights have been lonely without you."

The husky admission turned her bones to water. Weak with a passion suddenly too powerful to fight, Georgia closed her eyes and melted against him. How could she deny him when she heard in his voice the same ache, the same loneliness she had suffered?

With hot, tingling kisses, he explored the curve of her cheek, the softness of her lashes, the arch of her brow, reminding her all too vividly of the time she had openly sought his loving. His mouth moved to her ear, his tongue searching, enflaming. Moaning, she pressed herself to him, hungry for more.

The feel of her small breasts against his chest was exquisite torture. Pulling her closer, he captured her mouth with his; passion flared, quick and hot, between them. There was no past, no angry words between them now, only a naked need so strong it blotted out the world.

Georgia whimpered as his teeth sank into her lower lip, her fingers clutching his thick, dark hair. Everywhere he touched, heat flared and raced along her skin. A burning hunger consumed her. How had she endured the last two months without his touch, his kiss?

Old memories stirred, chilling her. The desperation

of loneliness, the emptiness of the past two months haunted her. His memory already tramped the corridors of her mind and shared her bed. Slowly, insidiously, he was invading every corner of her life. Was she going to give him her heart, too, sentencing herself to a lifetime of bleak nights?

Wes felt the change in her almost immediately. His hold on her tightened, his hands tangled in her hair to keep her close. "Georgia, honey, don't shut me out," he groaned hoarsely. "What is it? What's wrong?"

Everything, she wanted to cry, but she couldn't get the words past the unexpected lump in her throat. His pull on her heart terrified her. She had no willpower against the warmth of his smile, the hunger in his eyes. Yet she knew he would bring her nothing but heartache. He and her father were just alike—attracting female attention came as easy to them as breathing. Like her father, Wes would hurt her, but, God help her, that didn't seem to matter when he touched her. What was she going to do?

Frustrated, Wes stared at her tortured eyes, a frown darkening his brow, an unfamiliar feeling of helplessness gripping him. He had to find a way to fight her demons, her fears, or she would never be completely his. "There's no need to be nervous about tonight," he told her firmly, lifting her chin until their eyes met. "You don't have to tell your father anything you don't want to."

"It's not that. It's just . . ." She faltered, words escaping her. How could she possibly make him understand? "Wes . . . this isn't easy for me. I'm . . . scared."

"Of your father?" he asked in surprise. He hadn't thought she was afraid of anything. "Honey, you're a grown woman. You don't answer to your father anymore."

"No. I—"

He hugged her, cutting off her explanation. "Quit worrying. I'll be right there with you. No one's going to hurt you."

No one but you, she wanted to cry. But when she saw the concern in his dark brown eyes, the worry, the words died before ever reaching her lips. She sighed. "I know. I'll just be glad when it's over."

She dressed in a black-and-white, raw-silk sheath. The black, scalloped yoke and sleeves were a dramatic, sophisticated contrast to her fair skin, giving her a cool, untouchable look that safely concealed her insecure heart. Her face was pale, her eyes haunted, but when she added a bold dash of red lipstick to her mouth and diamonds to her ears she had a little more sparkle. She pinned her hair up in a loose chignon and reached for the doorknob. When cool air touched her naked back, she realized she hadn't zipped her dress. Impatiently, she pulled the zipper up, only to groan in disgust when it came to a sudden halt halfway up her back. "Damn!" Contorting her body, she tugged at the small tab between her shoulderblades, but it stubbornly refused to budge.

Cursing roundly, she pulled until her arms ached before finally jerking open the bathroom door and stepping into the bedroom, a scowl darkening her emerald eyes. "Wes, I need some help. I . . ."

The words died in her throat at the sight of him calmly tucking his shirttail into his unzipped black slacks. He looked up in time to catch her open-mouthed stare and grinned. "What's the problem?" he asked, finishing his task with an economy of movement, the sound of his zipper loud in the suddenly quiet room.

Georgia whirled, her cheeks burning. "My zipper. It's stuck."

He laughed softly and walked over to her stiff figure, his eyes feasting on the tempting skin of her naked back. He knew he should concentrate on the zipper, but he couldn't drag his hungry gaze from her skin. Just one touch, he promised himself, but when his fingers lightly traced her spine, she jumped, startled. "Easy, baby," he soothed in a deep rasp. "If you behave yourself, we won't have anything to worry about."

"Me?" she squeaked, his fingers searing her skin. "I haven't done anything."

"You got your zipper stuck," he reminded her with a low chuckle. Damn, she was beautiful! And so remote —at least on the surface. But he knew there were fires in her; he'd felt the heat. He longed to feel it again, to strip her clothes from her, and with them her cool reserve, to toss her on the bed and prove to her once and for all that she was his. But not yet. She wasn't ready.

The zipper slid into place. On a soft sigh, Georgia relaxed, then nearly choked with surprise when Wes nuzzled her nape, delighting her senses with the intoxicating warmth of his nearness. Too late, she stiffened, but his hands had already captured her shoulders to hold her in front of him. "Why don't we cancel dinner and stay here?" he growled against her skin. "I don't want to share you tonight."

A dizzy rush of desire overwhelmed her, and for one tense moment she couldn't move. When she finally pulled away and turned to face him she hid her shaking hands behind her back. Her eyes met his unflinchingly. "I'm not going to hop into bed with you just because we're getting married, Wes. There has to be more to our relationship than sex."

Irritated by her withdrawal, he had to curb the desire to snatch her back into his arms. "Isn't it enough that I want you more than any other woman I've ever known?"

"No," she whispered. "It isn't."

"Then what do you want?"

"Time. Time for us to develop a love life instead of a sex life. Time to fall in love." She saw the protest forming on his lips and hastily cut him off. "I know. You don't know if you can love me. Just don't veto the idea without giving us a chance."

No ultimatums were given, but Wes knew that if he gave the wrong answer, she would walk away. And he couldn't lose her now. He nodded. "All right. We'll take it slow."

4

Dinner was not the disaster she had feared.

It did, however, get off to a shaky start when Georgia stepped into the restaurant and immediately spotted her father in the crowded room. The waitress, a vivacious redhead, was hanging onto his every word and blushing prettily as he turned on the charm. Georgia's smile slipped, her face suddenly pale. How many times had Wes teased her with that same slow grin? She had learned a long time ago that her father often told her what she wanted to hear. Did Wes do the same?

Wes immediately noted her tension. He frowned. "Relax, will you?" he hissed in her ear as they made their way across the room. "Nobody's going to feed you to the lions."

"You don't understand—" But it was too late for explanations. They arrived at the table, and her father rose to hug her, an affectionate grin spreading across his handsome face. "Georgia, honey, you look beautiful. Where have you been hiding yourself?"

Through shuttered eyes, Wes watched father and daughter embrace, shrewdly inspecting the older man. Marcus Dupree had aged well. His square face was open and relatively unlined except for the laugh lines radiating from his friendly blue eyes, and a quick smile constantly played about his lips. Only a smattering of gray touched his thick brown hair to subtly mark the passage of the years. He was the type of man who could draw a smile from just about anyone, and Wes liked him immediately. But Georgia's attitude puzzled him. Although she returned her father's loving greeting, Wes sensed a reserve in her that was completely at odds with the older man.

As soon as she was able, Georgia stepped out of her father's arms and drew Wes forward, her fingers clutching his arm. "Dad, I want you to meet Wesley Hayden. Wes, my father, Marcus Dupree." She swallowed and forced her next words out of a suddenly dry throat. "Wes is my . . ."

"Fiancé," Wes supplied helpfully when she hesitated, a wide grin splitting his face as he held out his hand to the older man. "It's a pleasure to meet you, Mr. Dupree."

"Marc," he said dazedly. "Call me Marc." He shook his head as if trying to clear it. "You should give a warning before you drop a bomb like that. You could give a man heart failure."

"Believe me, sir, that wasn't my intention. I wasn't sure Georgia would be able to tell you. She's had some trouble with that word."

"Don't I know it. I didn't think she'd ever get

married." He pumped the younger man's hand enthusiastically. "I don't know how you talked her into it, son, but congratulations."

"Dad—"

"Thank you," Wes replied, smoothly cutting off the warning he could see trembling on Georgia's lips. "She fought me every step of the way, but I finally convinced her."

Georgia's jaw clenched with irritation, temper darkening her eyes like threatening storm clouds. How dare they discuss her as if she weren't there! "Would you two like me to leave?" she asked sweetly, reminding them of her presence. "Then you can discuss me as much as you like."

A rueful twinkle sprang into her father's eyes. "Sorry, honey. I still can't believe you're engaged." He pulled out a chair for her while Wes took the one next to her. "How long have you known each other?"

"Three months," Wes replied, a wicked grin tugging at his mouth as he captured her hand and brought it to his lips. "But I went down for the count the first time I laid eyes on her."

Georgia choked back a disbelieving snort. "Where's Kurt?" she asked shakily. "I haven't seen him in weeks. Isn't he coming?"

"Relax, mother hen," a laughing voice said behind her. "I'm here, late as usual."

Georgia turned with a start, a cry of delight escaping her as she jumped up to hug her brother. She only had time to note his white shirt open at the neck and the camel sports coat stretched tight across his broad shoulders before she was enfolded in his powerful arms. Six-foot-four in his stocking feet, his large body was rock hard and intimidating, and so very, very reassuring.

She held him at arm's length, grinning as she saw his dimples deepening in a smile that had devastated more than one feminine heart. "And what's your excuse this time?" she teased. "Blonde, brunette, or redhead?"

He grinned. "What can I say? I'm a popular guy."

"And modest, too," she laughed. She saw his hazel eyes shift to Wes and hastily made the introduction. "Kurt, this is my fiancé, Wesley Hayden."

Surprise registered on the younger man's face for only a second before his narrowed eyes openly inspected Wes. Georgia found herself holding her breath; Kurt's approval was very important to her. But she needn't have worried. Kurt offered Wes his hand, a slow grin lighting his eyes. "Welcome to the family. Dad didn't tell me we had an engagement to celebrate or I might have been on time for once."

"He didn't know," Wes admitted, firmly returning his handshake. "All-American at LSU, right?" At Kurt's nod, Wes turned to Georgia. "You didn't tell me you had a star athlete in the family."

"That's not surprising," her father chuckled as they all settled comfortably around the table. "Georgia's not one to volunteer information. In fact, she never dropped a hint that she was serious about anyone."

Wes laughed softly, all the tenderness Georgia could ever hope to see in his eyes warming her. "I swept her off her feet before she knew what hit her. We're getting married as soon as I can make the arrangements."

Kurt whistled in surprise. "You don't waste any time."

"Not when I see something I want," he agreed solemnly, brushing her cheek with the back of his fingers.

Georgia hardly heard her father order champagne. Why was Wes doing this? she wondered dazedly. Of course he wanted her family to think they were in love, but he didn't have to touch her, to look at her as if they were the only two people in the world. It did crazy things to her heartbeat. Suddenly feeling out of her depth, she turned hurriedly to her brother. "How's the team going to be this year, Kurt?"

Football immediately took over the conversation, and Georgia sighed in relief. She wasn't really surprised to discover Wes was as knowledgeable about the sport as her brother, and she listened in fascination as they discussed everything from high school to pro ball. Georgia occasionally joined in the conversation— she had, after all, kept up with Kurt's career—but she was distracted by her father. Already his eyes were roving to the other tables, checking out the women, searching for friends, nodding charmingly to those who caught his eye. Couldn't he just this once pretend he was giving his undivided attention to his family? What would Wes think?

But Wes hadn't noticed. A white-hot pain stabbed her in the heart as she watched Wes slowly look around the room. How could he do this to her? Did he actually expect her to sit meekly at his side while he made a fool of her? The hell she would! She opened her mouth to tell him exactly what she thought of him, but the waitress arrived with their meal, and her chance was gone. She stared at her shrimp in distaste, her appetite nonexistent, only to look up to find Wes's narrowed eyes also on her plate. Surprised, she watched him inspect her father's and Kurt's food before glancing at his own. Realization hit her like a bolt of lightning, and she grinned, relaxing for the first time that evening. Underneath the table, her foot nudged his. When he turned to her in surprise, she teased, "What are you doing? Checking out the competition?"

Sheepish laughter sparkled deep in his eyes. "Maybe."

"How do they measure up?"

"Actually, this place is pretty good," he admitted. "But it'd be better if they had some Creole dishes on the menu."

Georgia grimaced. "You could eat jambalaya for breakfast."

"Now you're talking," he agreed. "That even beats cold pizza."

"Anything beats cold pizza!"

"What's the name of your restaurant?" Kurt asked. Upon learning it was Sam's Place, he laughed. "You're kidding. That's my favorite restaurant."

The rest of the evening passed amicably, but Georgia couldn't help sighing in relief when they finally rose to leave. All her fears about Wes's wandering eye had proven to be groundless, and she had, in fact, been surprised by his attentiveness. She had felt the almost physical touch of his eyes throughout the evening, stroking her, caressing her, until awareness crackled like electricity between them. She was tense, on edge, anxious about the coming night, and she knew Kurt had picked up on it.

Wes touched her shoulder, frowning when she jumped in surprise. She was as nervous as a cat. "Are you all right?" he asked in concern.

She nodded, fighting the inexplicable urge to walk into his arms. "I guess I'm just tired," she said weakly.

"Then let's go home."

For once she didn't struggle. It was so much easier to let Wes take charge, to let him steer her toward the restaurant exit and not worry why it felt so right to have his hand at the back of her waist. She didn't protest even when her father stopped suddenly, his eyes drawn to a woman seated at a nearby table. "There's Elizabeth Striker. I haven't seen her in years." He turned to Georgia. "Excuse me for a minute, honey. She's seen me, and it would be rude to walk out without speaking to her."

"Of course," Georgia replied. He would never change and, suddenly, it didn't matter. "Take as long as you like. Wes and I have to get back to the apartment. There's still a lot to do before we leave tomorrow."

He hesitated only briefly before giving her a quick hug. "All right." He offered Wes his hand. "Take care of my little girl," he said gruffly.

"I will, sir," Wes promised him, slipping his arm around Georgia's waist before she could protest. "If she'll let me."

Her father laughed softly. "You're going to have your hands full. She's pretty independent."

"That's an understatement if there ever was one," Kurt chuckled, teasing affection in his eyes as they fell on his sister. "She's been ordering me around ever since I can remember."

Georgia knew they were only teasing, but she couldn't help the hurt that burned her eyes. They were making her sound like a shrew. She blinked back tears and ignored the two younger men to give her father a kiss. "Go talk to Elizabeth, Dad. I'm going home."

Wes and Kurt caught up with her outside, and Kurt immediately put his arms around her to hold her close. "Come on, sis. Don't be mad at me. I was only teasing, and it's not like you to be so sensitive."

"I know," she admitted thickly, suddenly clinging to him, her eyes hot with unshed tears. How could she explain the fears that swamped her? Her life was changing too quickly and somehow she was losing control. "Chalk it up to prewedding jitters."

"I think it's more than that," he replied quietly. Over her head, his eyes met Wes's. "When's the baby due?"

Georgia stiffened. "Kurt—"

"February," Wes replied.

The younger man's arms tightened around Georgia, his gaze direct, fierce with concern. "You'd better take good care of her, Wes. She's the only sister I've got."

Wes watched the turbulent emotions cloud Georgia's eyes on the way home, and he tightened his hands on the steering wheel in growing frustration. Tonight had explained a hell of a lot to him. Marcus Dupree hadn't fooled him for a second with his charming manners. Oh, he was friendly and easy to like. But he didn't love easily. He liked his freedom way too much to let anyone, especially his family, curtail his activities. And he was obviously the one who had taught Georgia to guard her heart to avoid pain.

Kurt, however, was another matter. He gave Georgia the security of his love freely, and she openly returned it. And Kurt had actually had the gumption to threaten him! Wes grinned wryly. He wasn't one to take threats lightly, and he certainly wasn't stupid enough to argue with a six-four, two-hundred-and-twenty-pound linebacker.

By the time they arrived at the apartment anxiety had twisted Georgia's nerves into knots. She shivered and hurriedly switched on all the living-room lights before going to the kitchen, all the while avoiding Wes's eyes. She pulled a cardboard box from the pantry, but nearly dropped it when she turned and found Wes standing in the doorway watching her.

"What are you doing?" he demanded as she pulled open the door to a kitchen cupboard.

"Packing my china," she said as calmly as her suddenly stiff lips would allow.

"Leave it," he ordered in growing irritation. "The movers will do it."

She shook her head stubbornly. "This is the only thing I have that was my mother's, and I'm not taking any chances with it. I'm taking it with me."

"You can do it in the morning," Wes retorted just as stubbornly, pushing himself away from the doorjamb and swiftly coming to her side. Pulling her hands away from the china, he shut the cabinet door with a snap. His gaze traveled the contours of her face, skimming over her flushed cheeks, green eyes that sparkled with defiance, and soft, feminine lips that trembled ever so slightly. His irritation died. "Why don't you go to bed?" he suggested quietly, reaching out to push her hair behind her ears. "You're tired. I'll help you with this tomorrow."

His gentleness devastated her. Her eyes hastily shied away from his. "No, I . . ."

"Yes," he replied firmly. His hands came down on her shoulders to steer her into the living room.

"Wes—"

He swung her around to face him, tender amusement wrestling with exasperation when he saw the panic that gripped her. When would she quit fighting him? He lifted her chin and forced her to look at him. "You're thinking again, sweetheart, and you're coming up with all the wrong answers. Go to bed. I've got some reports to read over and it'll be hours before I go to bed."

Tears burned her eyes, her throat. She hadn't expected him to understand. "I . . . you're right," she whispered. "I am tired. Good night."

With a tenderness that brought tears to her eyes, he bent to brush her lips with his. "Good night."

The weight of his arm around her waist woke her with the morning sun. Half asleep, she tugged at the unfamiliar warmth only to freeze as her hand closed over the hard strength of his arm. Her eyes flew open, her heart knocking against her ribs as awareness washed over her. Wes's warm breath caressed her neck, and the heat from his body scorched her back like a furnace. Without quite realizing what she was doing, her fingers slid down the sinewy muscles of his arm, loving the texture of his skin. Her mind balked at her madness, but she couldn't stop herself from hugging his arm against her waist. Just a few more minutes, she promised herself. She needed his closeness, his warm skin heating her, and for these few quiet moments she couldn't worry about the past or future.

The arm about her tightened suddenly to pull her

back against his firm, masculine chest, and with a start, Georgia realized she was the only one clothed. "Good morning," he murmured huskily, nuzzling the nape of her neck.

"Good morning," she choked, weakly closing her eyes as his hand flattened on her stomach and slid to rest just below her breast. Her heart did a crazy flip-flop, and she knew she had to get out of that bed fast. She tugged at the arm that was suddenly like a steel band around her. "Let go, Wes. I want to get up."

"Are you sure you're not going to kick me out of the bed again?" he teased as he lightly bit her earlobe. Desire shot through him at the sound of the muffled moan she couldn't suppress. He buried his face in her hair and groaned as her clean, delicate fragrance swirled about him. "Umm, you smell delicious. You should wake up in my arms every morning."

"Don't—"

Her denial tore through him like a rusty knife. Sweet Jesus, how could she do this to him? Didn't she know she was tearing him apart? He stopped her struggles with a touch, his hands gently forcing her down until she was flat on her back. His black eyes bored into hers. "Do you really want me to stop?" he demanded roughly.

Georgia stared at him, her eyes wide and searching as they roamed his face. The pain, the need she saw reflected in his eyes, etched in the tight, unyielding lines of his face, reproached her, and her protests died on her lips. Deep inside her the shell that protected her too vulnerable heart cracked, and sudden realization shook her to the depths of her being. She loved him.

Dear God, she loved him! She didn't even know how it had happened. He had laughed at her fears and touched her heart with his smile, his kiss, and the battle was lost. She loved him and he needed her. How could she possibly deny him what they both wanted? She melted, her body suddenly soft and pliant in his arms. "No," she sighed in a voice she hardly recognized. "Don't stop."

His eyes flared in surprise and he gathered her to him with a groan. His blood thundered at the sweetness of her response, and he had to fight the need to crush her against him and take her quickly. He had waited so long for her to come to him willingly, he wanted to savor every caress, every kiss. His body shook with the effort, but he clamped a tight lid on his desire and rolled to his side, taking her with him, his arms strong yet gentle as he cradled her against him. The feel of her body against his was sweet torture, and with a ragged sigh, he gave himself up to the need to reacquaint himself with her body's secrets.

Georgia quivered, the feel of his hair-roughened leg over hers making her weak with desire. How had she lived without him for all this time? she wondered dazedly, returning kiss for kiss, touch for touch until her pulses pounded crazily. The need to drive him slowly out of his mind with pleasure consumed her. She pulled his wandering mouth back to hers, and with a lazy sensuousness that devastated him, she traced the lines of his mouth before sinking her teeth gently into his lower lip. His growl of pleasure shot fire into her loins, and instinctively she pulled him closer before breaking off the kiss to explore his ear with a flick of her tongue. His response was quick and hard against her.

"Ah, sweetheart, you're playing with fire," he rasped thickly, finally giving in to temptation and crushing her against him.

Georgia gloried in the feel of his lean, sinewy muscles under her fingers, and at the touch of her hands on him, his control snapped. Abruptly he wrenched his mouth from hers and forged a trail of hot kisses down her throat to her breast, circling the peak slowly, torturously, before taking it into his mouth to be suckled hungrily. Her startled cry of pleasure enflamed him, and he gave her other breast the same lavish, loving treatment. Shudders wracked her slender body, and he growled in approval. She was going up in flames in his arms, and he loved it. "Do you know how much I need you? Don't make me wait any longer, sweetheart. I've got to have you."

Through Georgia's passion-clouded mind, his words echoed hollowly, coldly, and the fog strangling her reason suddenly lifted. He needed her. That was all. There were no tender promises of love, of undying devotion. She'd thought she could accept that, but the thought of having only his desire chilled her. It wasn't enough. She had to have all or nothing.

She pushed him away, and before Wes could question her change in mood, she had slipped free of him. Backing away from the bed, she held her robe in front of her suddenly shaking body, her tortured eyes meeting his fleetingly before shying away. "We can't spend the morning in bed," she said hoarsely. "We've got a lot to do before we can head back to New Orleans."

The bathroom door slammed loudly in the suddenly quiet room, the click of the lock like a slap in the face. Wes swore viciously and threw back the sheet, pulling on jeans and a black T-shirt, his eyes murderous as they lingered on the door. Damn it to hell, what had gone wrong? One minute she had been purring in his arms and the next scurrying away like a scared rabbit. His body burned with need, and he'd be damned if he was going to let her get away with this. He stomped over to the taunting closed door and pounded on it angrily. "Open this door, Georgia!" he ordered. "We have to talk." Mocking silence answered him and he hit the door again with a clenched fist. "Damn it, did you hear me? I said—"

She jerked open the door. "I heard you the first time," she answered coolly. "I'm not deaf." She met his gaze unflinchingly. She wasn't surprised that he wanted to throttle her, but she couldn't let things go any farther.

The ice was back in place; it frosted her eyes and dripped from every word, chilling him. She was hiding behind that frozen wall again, and he wouldn't, couldn't let her. "Would you mind telling me what this is all about?"

His voice was just as cold as hers, his face grim and ruthless, stripped of the polished veneer that usually covered the tough, hard side of him. She had pushed him to this, and she felt miserable. "I'm sorry," she finally managed huskily. "I never intended to let things go so far. I . . . I just don't want to get hurt, Wes."

His eyes were fierce as they swept over her, but self-reproach stabbed him when he saw the strain around her soft mouth, the pain that darkened her emerald eyes. His anger cooled. He had promised her time and he was already trying to break his word. But it was getting harder and harder to keep his hands to himself. He reached out to cup her cheek. "No, I'm sorry. I gave you my word I wouldn't rush you, but I want you so badly, I keep forgetting." He gently caressed her lips with his thumb. "Come on, let's go to work."

She couldn't believe that he could forget so easily, but he did. By midafternoon everything was packed, all the small, personal items she wanted to take with her safely stowed in the car. Georgia stood in the living room and stared at the stripped apartment, the empty end tables and bare walls, and instinctively knew she was looking at the end of a chapter of her life. The future yawned uncertainly before her, and even if she eventually came back to Baton Rouge, nothing would ever be the same again.

Wes stood in the doorway, watching her memorize every detail of the apartment. He ached to take her in his arms, to reassure her that she had nothing to fear, but after what had happened this morning he was reluctant to touch her, reluctant to test the promise he had made so freely. He shoved his hands in his pockets, away from temptation. "That seems to be about it. Are you ready to go?"

She nodded. There was no point in lingering. But when her gaze brushed a lonely geranium that sat in the living-room window memories tugged at her heart. She walked over to pick it up, her arms tightening around the clay pot. "David gave this to me when I moved in here. I have to call him to explain."

For some reason he couldn't fathom, her concern for his friend's feelings irritated him. He reached for the phone. "I'll do it. After all, I'm partly responsible."

"No! Wait—"

But it was too late. The call had already gone through. "David!" Wes greeted him. "How's it going?"

"Oh, you know how it is," David replied lightly. "I've been keeping my nose to the grindstone. Hey, where are you? Here in town?"

Wes's dark, enigmatic eyes met Georgia's, holding her captive. "As a matter of fact I am. I'm at Georgia's apartment, but we're going to start back to New Orleans in a few minutes. We're getting married."

"Married!" David yelped in surprise. "You? Come on, Wes, you're pulling my leg."

"Believe me, I wouldn't kid about marriage," he replied dryly. He saw Georgia wince and cursed his foolish tongue. He hadn't meant it the way she was obviously taking it, but she'd never believe that now. Damn, when did things get so complicated?

"I didn't even think you two were speaking to each other," his friend continued, blissfully unaware of the bad memories his words were dredging up. "Georgia never would speak of it, but I got the distinct impression she hated your guts. And now she's going to marry you? Come on, Wes, what's going on?"

"I told you. We're getting married. *This* week."

Even from several feet away, Georgia could hear David's cry of dismay. She snatched the phone out of Wes's unsuspecting hand and shot him a quelling glance that should have curled his hair. Despite the fact that he was her boss, David had been a good friend to her, and she owed him nothing less than the truth. Ignoring Wes's scowling face, she said, "David, I'm sorry about this. I'd like to give you two weeks' notice, but I can't. I'm . . . pregnant," she explained, stumbling over the word, "so Wes and I are getting married immediately."

"Are you sure this is what you want?" David asked in concern. "Don't do this just because of the baby, Georgia. If you're going to marry him, make sure it's for the right reasons."

"I am," she said softly, achingly aware of Wes's disapproval as he seemed to hover over her. She loved him; she had probably loved him since that first day he had sat on her desk and grinned at her, and that made everything all right. It wasn't the perfect relationship, but he would be a part of her life, hers to take care of, to touch, to love, at least as much as he would let her. "Don't worry about me, David, everything will be fine. But I might want to work after the baby is born. Could you arrange a leave of absence for me until I know what I want to do?"

"Of course. Take all the time you need. And keep in touch. Okay?"

"Okay," she agreed huskily. Without another word, she handed the phone back to Wes and walked out.

They were married three days later. Without fanfare, without any family or friends present, Georgia stood before a justice of the peace, a stranger, and promised to love and honor Wesley Hayden for the rest of her life. Her fingers trembled in his, but her voice was strong, and she couldn't help wondering if marrying her meant anything to Wes. He wasn't making a commitment to her; he was giving his child a name. And, in return, he had grudgingly signed the prenuptial agreement she had insisted upon. She tried to keep her emotions in check, to let the coldness that gripped her heart freeze her tears, but she had set an impossible task for herself. Wes played the loving groom to the hilt, kissing her passionately after the ceremony, holding her close, caressing her with his eyes, but his loverlike attention brought Georgia no joy. Her wedding would have been perfect if only it hadn't been necessary.

5

A week later, the sun was just creeping over the horizon when Wes woke with Georgia in his arms. Her breath was slow and easy, sweet upon his chest where she lay nestled against him, her soft, silky blond curls tickling his nose. For a long, quiet moment he studied her, slowly inspecting every inch of her that was left exposed by her lacy white nightgown, enjoying this freedom to gaze at her to his heart's content. Almost imperceptibly his arms tightened as she stirred in her sleep, the intoxicating fragrance of her teasing his senses, coaxing his body into hardness.

He couldn't find the strength to let her go. Just five more minutes, he promised himself. Five more minutes of torturing himself with the feel of her curled against him, seeking his warmth, holding him close. Once he left their bed it would be another long day without her, cold, empty hours during which they acted more like polite strangers than husband and wife. She seemed content with the status quo while his body burned for her, and his only recourse was to throw himself into work so that there would be no opportunities to drag her off to bed. But always, regardless of what he was doing, he waited for the night.

In the night her body betrayed her mind. In her sleep she always ended up in his arms.

When holding her was no longer enough he knew he couldn't jeopardize the fragile truce they had so carefully erected during the last week. She wanted time before they slipped back into a physical relationship, and somehow he would find the strength to give it to her. With a muffled groan, he left their bed and walked naked into the bathroom.

Georgia woke with a start, disoriented, her sleep-clouded eyes lingering on the empty side of the bed. Despair filled her heart. She knew she had slept in his arms. Again. And she hadn't even known when he came to bed.

Blinking back tears, she rolled onto her back and stared blindly at the ceiling. How much more of this could she take? He spent all his time at the restaurant, leaving her to contend with the long, aimless hours of the day. And, in desperation, she had learned every nook and cranny of his house, the contents of every drawer, every closet. She weeded the flower beds, filled the pantry and refrigerator with food, and cleaned the house from top to bottom. But it didn't help. She still had too much time to think. And always her thoughts were the same.

Wes was polite. And distant. They shared a bed and little else. Instead of trying for the emotional closeness she needed, he had completely walled himself off from her. She carried his name and his child, yet she still wasn't a part of his life.

Accepting his aloofness wouldn't be nearly as painful for her if she didn't love him to distraction. His absence during the day left her empty and lonely, and the thought of spending the rest of her life without him terrified her. She no longer wanted her freedom, her precious independence. They were meaningless without Wes by her side. Somehow she had to win his love.

But first she had to break through that wall of reserve he had built around himself since their wedding. She heard a movement downstairs and glanced sharply at the digital clock on the bedside table. There were still a few minutes left before he would leave for work. Maybe they could talk.

She hastily got dressed and hurried downstairs. She reached the last step just as he started to walk out the front door. "Wes . . . can I talk to you for a minute?"

Her breathless question caught him off guard and he turned in surprise, his breath catching in his throat at the sight of her. Damn, but she was beautiful with her hair tumbling about her face and her cheeks aglow from her run down the stairs. A quick rush of desire coursed through his body, staggering him with its fierceness, and he knew he had to get out of there before his baser side damned his good intentions and found release in her body. He scowled. "I've got a meeting in fifteen minutes. You'll have to make it fast."

His indifference hurt, and Georgia stared at him in bewilderment. Who was this handsome stranger in the light gray summer suit, with his cold, remote eyes and grim countenance? "I won't hold you up," she said stiffly. "I was just wondering if you had any openings at the restaurant. I'm going crazy cooped up here in the house, and we never see each other anymore. If we worked together—"

"No." Never! She couldn't have any idea what she was asking of him. She already tortured his nights with her nearness, driving him half mad with her delicious body. His dreams, his fantasies were becoming an obsession, and he wouldn't court disaster by inviting her into the one haven he had left that was still relatively free of her presence—his work. "I'm sorry. There aren't any openings."

"But you're the owner!"

"Would you like me to fire someone just to make room for you?"

"Of course not!"

He reached for the doorknob. "Then you'll have to find some other way to keep yourself occupied." His eyes locked with hers. "Dinner at the usual time?"

"Yes, I suppose so," she replied with a marked lack of enthusiasm, but he didn't even notice. He was gone.

The silence in the house was heavy, oppressive, thick with words left unsaid, and Georgia found she could no longer ignore the nagging worry that had been bothering her for days. Was there something wrong with her? Was that why Wes no longer pressed for a more intimate relationship? She stared at her reflection in the hall mirror, her eyes critical.

Pregnancy hadn't changed her all that much. She was still slim, her skin clear, the soft curves and planes of her body the same as they had always been. She knew Wes wasn't totally unaffected by her presence. In unguarded moments she had caught his eyes on her, devouring her before he would invariably find an excuse to leave. If he still wanted her, why was he avoiding her?

The pounding of the front-door knocker reverberated rudely through her musings, but Georgia welcomed the distraction. She was tired of talking to herself.

Jenny Prescott stood on the front steps, her auburn hair blazing in the morning sun, a white tank top and snug-fitting jeans hugging her slim body. Two days after her marriage Georgia had opened her door to discover Jenny on the steps, asking to see Wes. He, of course, had been at the restaurant, and the two women had been extremely wary of each other, the memory of their first meeting still vivid in their minds. Jenny, sensing Georgia's suspicions, had taken the bull by the horns and quickly assured Georgia she wasn't after her husband, that they were just friends and she'd like to be Georgia's friend, too. Georgia had welcomed the offer.

She pulled the door wider. "You're just the person I need to talk to. Want a cup of coffee?"

Jenny frowned at Georgia's solemn expression. "Sure. What's up?" she asked as she followed her into the kitchen and settled herself at the table while Georgia started to make the coffee. "I almost ran into Wes outside, but I don't think he even saw me."

"I'm not surprised," Georgia sighed. "He's been in his own little world lately, and unfortunately, I'm not a part of it."

"Maybe he's just working too hard."

Georgia shook her head. "No," she said quietly. "That's just his excuse to get away from me. He's already feeling trapped."

"Has he said that?" her friend asked in surprise.

"He hasn't had to. But you know Wes and I only got married because of the baby."

"I know that's what you said," Jenny countered dryly.

A slim brow shot up in surprise. "You don't believe me?"

"I didn't say that. I just think there's more to your shotgun wedding than you're admitting." Her sapphire eyes were kind but determined when they met Georgia's. "You love him, don't you?"

Georgia hesitated. "Yes." Unable to sit still, she jumped up to pace restlessly about the kitchen, finally coming to a stop in front of the French doors that opened onto the patio. She stared out blindly. "But Wes only married me to give the baby a name. He doesn't love me."

"How do you know?" Jenny demanded. "Has he told you he doesn't?"

"No, but he hasn't told me he does."

"He probably won't." When Georgia turned to look at her in surprise Jenny smiled wryly. "We're talking about Wesley Hayden here, remember? He doesn't exactly wear his heart on his sleeve. He's a cautious man, and for as long as I've known him, I've never known him to let anyone get close enough to hurt him. That's what you're up against."

"I don't want to hurt him," Georgia cried, the tight control she'd kept on her emotions suddenly gone. "He won't even let me get close enough to love him," she admitted huskily. "He spends all his time at the restaurant, so I thought if I could find something to do in his business, I would at least get to see him more. But he flatly refused to even consider it. If I didn't know better, I'd swear he was avoiding me."

"So you're giving up? Just like that?"

"What else can I do? Force myself on him?"

"That's certainly one option." Jenny laughed. "He needs you more than he'll ever admit. If you want your marriage to work, you're going to have to worm your way into his life whether he wants you to or not."

Taking Jenny's advice to heart, Georgia arrived at the restaurant the following afternoon after the lunch crowd had dispersed, only to find the large, airy dining room empty except for several white-coated waiters and a few customers who lingered over the remains of lunch. Standing just inside the entranceway, Georgia smoothed the skirt of her mint-green sundress and allowed herself a few minutes to appreciate the utter simplicity of the restaurant's decor. An antique mahogany bar dominated one end of the room, its dark wood glistening from the tender care of loving hands, the beveled mirrors behind it sparkling with reflected images of glassware and liquor. Round tables were dispersed uniformly throughout the dining area, their white linen tablecloths spotless, the hurricane lamps that sat in the middle of each adding a touch of old-world charm. And, overhead, ceiling fans murmured quietly, discreetly stirring up a gentle breeze.

Wes's touch was everywhere, his insistence on excellence obvious. Sam's Place was an unqualified success, but Wes could no longer use it as an excuse to avoid her. Purposefully, she headed for his office.

When she stepped into the restaurant's executive suite, Wes's secretary looked up from her typing, her blue eyes sharp behind the thick lenses of her glasses. Sylvia Mason had been with Wes for years, running his office with an iron hand, guarding the door to his inner sanctum like a bulldog, and generally making herself indispensable. She had little time for nonsense; she seldom took the world lightly, and Georgia secretly thought the older woman had missed her calling as a drill sergeant.

Georgia smiled, though, as she greeted her. "How are you today, Sylvia?"

"Busy."

Georgia grimaced. So much for small talk. "Is Wes busy? I need to talk to him. . . ."

"He's not in," the secretary interrupted. "He's out checking sites for the new restaurant. Is there something I can help you with?"

"No . . . thank you. I guess I'll just have to wait till I see him at dinner."

But dinner would probably be too late, she thought morosely as she shut the office door behind her. He wouldn't be in any mood to listen. He never was. It was a stupid idea, anyway, thinking she could force her way into his daily activities without his permission. He'd never allow it.

But how could he stop her? a tiny voice countered. There was, after all, more than one way to skin a cat, and if Wes didn't want her working with him, there were other ways to involve herself in his life.

She stormed into the kitchen like a small whirlwind, and Mark Reynolds blinked in surprise, the knife he held clattering to the stainless-steel counter at the sight of her set face. "Mrs. Hayden! What's wrong?"

Too late, Georgia remembered that the kitchen was

the chef's domain, and it went against protocol to just come barging in like a fishwife. Some chefs were notoriously temperamental, and she had no idea if Mark Reynolds fell into that category. If he burned dinner because of her, Wes would have a fit. She hastily stepped back against the kitchen door. "Mr. Reynolds, I'm sorry. I should have knocked."

"Don't be ridiculous." He laughed. "Since you're the boss's wife, you've certainly got a right to come into the kitchen. What can I do for you?"

Georgia grinned, instantly liking this young man with his curly, black hair and the perpetual twinkle in his bright blue eyes. He certainly didn't look old enough to be a chef, but she'd tasted his cooking, and it was heavenly. She stepped away from the door. "Well, now that you mention it, I could use your help." At the inquisitive quirk of his brow, she smiled sheepishly. "I was hoping you might teach me to cook."

"You don't know how?"

"Don't sound so horrified," she frowned. "I was too busy to learn when I was in school, and later it just wasn't worth it for one person. Anyway, I like TV dinners and pot pies."

"Some people will eat anything."

"Wes won't."

"Aha!" he crowed triumphantly. "Now we come to the reason for the cooking lessons. Wes doesn't like your cooking."

She hesitated to admit that Wes had never even tried her cooking, and said instead, "It isn't that he doesn't like it; he just prefers yours. And since I don't want to eat every meal out, I thought if I learned to cook Wes's favorite dishes, he might consent to eat at home occasionally. He spends too much time here."

"I agree," he said, surprising her. "When would you like to start?"

"Yesterday, but I'll settle for today. If that's convenient for you," she tacked on hopefully.

He handed her an apron, laughter dancing in his eyes. "Today it is."

Thirty minutes later Georgia stood before the huge commercial stove that dominated one wall of the kitchen, an oversize apron tied around her waist, doubt etching her brow as she stared at the contents of the pot in front of her. "Are you sure I'm doing this right? This looks horrible."

"I don't know what you're complaining about," Mark protested. "I'm doing the dirty work for you."

She looked over her shoulder to where he sat at the butcher-block table in the center of the kitchen, unable to suppress a delicate shudder as she watched him stuff crawfish heads with a mixture of bread, scallions, and seasonings for the bisque she was attempting to cook. She hastily averted her eyes. "I'll never be able to do that without gagging."

He chuckled and went to place a tray of the stuffed heads in the oven. "Sure you will. How's the bisque coming?" He looked over her shoulder at the mixture of flour and oil she was stirring, a frown darkening his brows as his eyes returned to hers accusingly. "You haven't been stirring this continuously. I think you've scorched it."

"Oh, I'll never be able to do this!" she said in disgust, suddenly discouraged. She threw down her spoon and reached for the ties of her apron. "This is a total waste of time. I'm a lawyer, not a cook, and there's no way I can become a gourmet chef in one easy lesson. Or even ten."

Mark reached over to turn off the flame under the bisque. "This is hardly gourmet, Georgia, but there are less complicated dishes. Would you rather start with something easier?"

"No. I—"

Without warning, the kitchen door swung open, a burst of laughter cutting off her next words, her heart skipping a beat at the sight of the man and woman standing in the doorway, shared laughter warming their eyes. Sarah Gardner and Wes. Why did the sight of her husband with the restaurant hostess hurt her so much? Surely she wasn't jealous of the fact that Wes was laughing and joking with the sophisticated blonde, something he hadn't done with Georgia since they were married? No, jealousy was too mild a word for what she was feeling. She'd been slaving over a hot stove for *her* husband, and maybe it was time she let Wes and everyone else know whom he belonged to.

Warily, Wes watched her approach, his eyes lingering on the gentle sway of her hips beneath the huge apron before slowly traveling up every curve and contour of her delightful figure. He stopped at her mouth, uneasiness creeping into his stomach at the sight of her sudden flashing smile. She didn't fool him for a minute. She was furious, and for the life of him, he didn't know what he'd done to spark the fury in her eyes. He studied her thoughtfully, unexpected laughter flirting with his mouth when she shot Sarah a murderous glare from beneath lowered lashes. He grinned. She was jealous!

At the sight of that grin, Georgia felt like kicking

him. So he thought it was funny, did he? When she got through with him, every woman within a hundred miles would know he was no longer available. Lifting her chin, she walked right up to him and slid her arms around his neck. "I've been waiting for you, darling," she purred in the most seductive voice she could manage. "The house was lonely without you." And before she allowed herself time to think about the wisdom of her actions, she laid a kiss on him that was guaranteed to knock his socks off.

Wes loved it. He took full advantage of the situation, and somewhere in the kiss, Georgia lost the initiative. When his arms dragged her close and his tongue hungrily searched for the secrets of her mouth, desire warmed her blood until she was weak with longing. She forgot her need to strike back at him, forgot the other occupants of the kitchen, the world. The ice in her melted under a blaze of heat.

Her response went to Wes's head like a potent liquor, and just for an instant, he couldn't keep from crushing her to him, taking everything she offered so sweetly. But even then he wasn't completely lost to their surroundings. Slowly, reluctantly, he broke off the kiss, though it was damn hard when she swayed toward him. Self-deprecating humor sprang into his dark eyes as his body throbbed with need. Damn, her timing was lousy!

Through passion-clouded eyes, Georgia saw him hastily swallow laughter, and she fell back to earth with a jolt. Mortified, she saw Mark and Sarah's understanding smiles and could have died right there on the spot. Hot color flooded her cheeks. She should have known she couldn't play such a dangerous game with Wes. Her senses would betray her every time.

Suddenly anxious to escape, she slipped away from him before he realized her intentions and fled to the swinging double doors that led to the dining room. "I need to talk to you when you have a few minutes," she told him stiffly. "I'll wait for you in your office."

He joined her almost immediately, slipping into the room on silent feet, coming up behind her as she stood gazing unseeingly out the window. He frowned at the tired droop of her shoulders, the faint violet shadows under her eyes. She was thinner than she should be, and he knew from the long, endless nights he'd held her in his arms that she wasn't sleeping well. Had marriage done this to her? Was she that unhappy? "What did you want to talk about?" he asked quietly.

"Us."

A dark brow shot up in surprise. "What about us?"

How could he be so dense? she wondered in agitation. Did he actually think their marriage was normal? "What about us?" she repeated. "There is no us! Can't you see that? I only see you for lunch and dinner, and even then you hardly say anything. I can't take seven more months of this."

"Seven more months of what?"

"Of . . . of this marriage of convenience!"

"Well, I'm glad to hear it," he chuckled suddenly, "because it's killing me!"

Georgia wanted to kill him. At that moment she could think of nothing more satisfying than wrapping her fingers around his neck and wiping that stupid grin from his handsome face. But what good would it do when he obviously took their problems so lightly? "Just forget I said anything," she choked.

But Wes had no intention of letting her drop the subject. He caught her before she'd taken two steps. "Hold it," he ordered gruffly as he pulled her back against him and wrapped his arms around her waist. Her softness seduced him, the remembered feel of her beneath him torturing his senses, and he cradled her against him. "I'm sorry I laughed, but I don't want to forget this. Are you trying to tell me you want me to make love to you?"

Her heart jumped against her ribs. "No!" Couldn't he see that sex wasn't their problem? If the marriage was going to work at all, the giving couldn't be all one-sided. "We have to make some changes in this crazy marriage of ours."

"Name them," he growled.

She took a deep breath. "I don't know where I belong in your life," she said quietly. "I don't even know if I'm part of it. I never see you. We never talk. You spend all your time working, but I can't be part of that. I can't take any more of this . . . loneliness." Her voice broke. "When I was ten years old," she finally said, "I swore I wouldn't follow in my mother's footsteps. And I won't, not even for you."

"And what does your mother have to do with this?" he asked, his mouth against her hair.

Unexpected tears thickened her voice. "My mother put up with a hell of a lot from my father. She was a housewife, and Dad was on the road a lot as a salesman. It seemed like Mom was always waiting for him to come home. Sometimes he didn't make it. And even when he was home, he gave other women more attention than he gave her."

Instinctively, he turned her in his arms and pulled her against his chest, his arms warm, comforting, and protective. For long moments he held her, stroking her hair, his murmured endearments easing the hurt.

Georgia wanted to stay that way forever, but she had to tell him of the fear that had been worrying her since she'd met him. "You and my father are a lot alike, Wes," she said quietly.

He stiffened. "And just what the hell do you mean by that?"

His outraged snarl stunned her, and, instinctively, she tried to step free of his arms, but his grip only tightened. "Wes . . . I . . . there's no need to get so upset. I wasn't criticizing."

"I'm sure you weren't, but you started this, so finish it."

"All right!" Defiance glittered in her eyes as she jerked free of his hold and stepped back to look him straight in the eye. "You and my father are both charming, and women just seem to naturally flock to you. Sometimes a wife gets in the way."

He stalked toward her, a predatory gleam deep in his eyes. "And you think that's why I won't let you work with me? Because you'd get in the way?"

She paled at the sight of the grim fury that hardened his face into that of a stranger. "No, I . . . I never said that," she denied in a whisper.

"No, but you were thinking it, so don't bother denying it." Like an eagle catching his prey, his fingers closed around her arms to snatch her up before him.

"Did it ever occur to you that I might have another reason for not giving you a job?"

"N–no."

The shakiness of her response reproached him and, startled, he realized he was holding her too tightly. With a muttered oath, he released her. "I'm sorry. I didn't mean to grab you, but I seem to lose all control around you." He drove his fingers impatiently through his dark hair. "Damn it, honey, how can you accuse me of being like your father? I'm not interested in other women. How could I be when you drive me wild?"

"You must be joking," she scoffed. "You haven't touched me since we were married."

"You made it clear you didn't want me to."

She winced. She had never stopped to consider how difficult the situation was for him. "So that's why you've been avoiding me."

"Do you think it's been easy for me to be around you and not touch you? Kiss you?" he rasped as he eliminated the distance between them in a single step. With a gentleness that touched her heart, he traced the curve of her brow, her cheek, her lips, with fingers that were not quite steady before following the path again with his mouth. "I want you, honey," he murmured against her trembling lips. "And just holding you at nights is driving me out of my mind. I've tried throwing myself into work, exercise, even cold showers. Nothing works. You're still with me every minute of the day and night. You've got to believe that."

She did. Because he had just described her own feelings for him. And because he had unwittingly described emotions that could only be called love. Her eyes sparkled like stars. "Since we've both been miserable, don't you think we should do something about it?"

He grinned. "What did you have in mind?"

"Well, for starters, you can come home for dinner. I'm tired of eating out."

6

When Georgia left the restaurant less than an hour later, her feet hardly touched the ground, and she didn't even notice the amused glances that were cast her way as she practically floated home. Wes loved her. Oh, he hadn't said so in so many words, but she had seen the naked emotion in his eyes and recognized it for what it was. Love. What a beautiful four-letter word.

Laughter danced in her veins like bubbles in a glass of champagne, and with a delighted grin, she realized she wasn't acting like her usual self. Ms. Dupree, the cool, sophisticated attorney, had never gone so far as to forget herself and let down her hair. Ah, but Mrs. Hayden was another matter entirely. Her husband loved her, and she was tickled to death by the news. With very little encouragement she would find herself swinging on a chandelier and shouting with joy. For the first time in her life she was high on love.

And tonight was going to be beautiful. They were no longer two strangers who seldom touched except in bed, and all the fantasies she had tortured herself with could at last come true. If she could get Wes to admit his love for her, the night would be perfect.

That, she wryly acknowledged, would be the hard part. He would fight her every step of the way, but she didn't plan to fight fair. He was her husband, she loved him with all of her heart, and she knew of only one way to get past his defenses to his real feelings. Seduction with a capital S.

The evening would start with a romantic dinner. After all, how complicated could that be? She was a woman of above-average intelligence, and anyone who could read could cook. And it wasn't as if she was leaving anything to chance. The menu was planned down to the last detail, and Mark Reynolds had assured her she would have no problems with the recipes he had given her. He had even helped her finish the crawfish bisque and boosted her confidence immeasurably with a pep talk that would have done Vince Lombardi proud.

She would, of course, need a very special dress to carry out her plans properly. When she stepped into the small dress shop located a few blocks from the house, Georgia had little doubt she would find the dress she was looking for. The question was, could she afford it? The shop catered to an elite group of wealthy society women who, no doubt, never blinked an eye at the astronomical prices of the merchandise. Georgia couldn't be quite so blasé, but it didn't cost to look.

She found it almost immediately. The design was

deceptively simple, almost plain, and on the hanger, it looked like nothing more than a wraparound with a crisscross bodice and a full, flowing skirt held together by a tie at the waist. But something urged her to try it on, and when she did, she was lost. A delicate rose hue, it was made of the finest silk and felt almost decadent against her skin. The neckline dipped daringly, revealing a less than maidenly view of her breasts, bringing a blush to her cheeks. Wes would love it. Without a second thought, she bought it.

By the time she arrived home she was running late, and she only had time to hang the new dress in her closet before she hurried downstairs to the kitchen. And from that point on nothing went right.

The chicken refused to brown until she was distracted by dreams of Wes and the coming evening, and when she came back to earth, it was too late. "Stupid bird," she muttered, disdainfully prodding an almost black leg with a fork. She couldn't possibly put this in the jambalaya, but it was the only chicken she had in the house and she didn't have time to go to the grocery store. Maybe Wes wouldn't notice it was slightly burned if she cut off the charred pieces.

Over half the chicken ended up in the garbage, but by the time the rest of the ingredients were in the pot, Georgia knew she couldn't disguise a disaster. Somehow it looked nothing like the jambalaya Mark made. Her eyes lingered on the brown onion bits that floated in the soupy mixture, and she wrinkled her pert nose in distaste. How the hell did you sauté onions anyway? she wondered in disgust as she wiped her sweaty brow with the back of her hand. She'd tried *three* times, and she still hadn't gotten it right. What else could go wrong?

The bread pudding and rum sauce she'd planned for dessert, were, thankfully, easier than the jambalaya, and by the time she put it in the oven and headed upstairs to shower and change, she was feeling more optimistic. She had never pretended to be a whiz in the kitchen, so Wes could hardly complain about her lack of domestic skills. And if the evening turned out the way she hoped, food would be the last thing on his mind.

When she finally slipped into her new dress anticipation glowed like a small fire in the depth of her eyes. Her dress was perfect, swirling about her legs with whispered sighs as she turned to make a last-minute check of her appearance in the dresser mirror. Georgia caught her breath in surprise, her eyes riveted to her reflected image. She hardly recognized the sensuous woman in the mirror. With her hair swept up into an artful disarray of curls and the rose silk clinging lovingly to every curve of her body, she looked like a seductress, and wickedly sinful. The curves of her breasts were clearly revealed by the low neckline, and it was blatantly obvious she wasn't wearing a bra. She grinned, sudden laughter breaking the spell that held her motionless before the mirror. If Wes could ignore her tonight, he needed help.

But Wes had no intention of ignoring her. He had just stepped through the front door when she appeared before him, a vision of loveliness with a welcoming smile on her soft lips and a drink in her hand.

Georgia flushed as his eyes devoured her, a sweet tide of longing sweeping through her as she saw need flare in the depths of his black eyes. She smiled, relief making her giddy. He wanted her as much as she wanted him. Impulsively, she reached up to fleetingly brush his lips with hers, but at the spark of electricity that shot through her, she reluctantly pulled back. They had all night, and she didn't want to rush one beautiful second of it. "Dinner's not quite ready," she said huskily as she handed him his drink. "You've got time for a shower."

Bemusedly, Wes swallowed his whiskey in one gulp, hardly tasting it, his senses intoxicated by her nearness. His mind reeled at the changes in her, and he couldn't resist the urge to discover just how deep they went. With infinite slowness, he traced the low neckline of her dress, his fingers shaking ever so slightly as they dipped under the material to linger on the full curves of her breasts and the scented valley in between, all the while watching for the least sign of coldness in her eyes. But a ragged breath was her only response, and satisfaction curled deep within him. "Would you mind telling me what's going on here?" he growled softly.

His fingers burned her skin, knocking her heart sideways until it pounded against her ribs, and Georgia knew he'd have to be blind not to see her reaction to his touch. But she wanted no misunderstandings. She lifted her eyes to his, her desire obvious. "I just wanted to show you what you've been missing by not coming home to dinner."

Laughter flickered in the shadows in his dark eyes. "I see." Almost as if by chance, his roving fingers moved to the tie at the side of her waist, his teeth flashing in a wicked grin. "And I suppose this sexy dress just happened to be lying around the house?"

"Well, not exactly," she hedged, her nose wrinkling

prettily. "I bought it this afternoon, and it cost the earth." She lifted wide, innocent eyes to his, vainly trying to stop the laughter that pulled at her mouth. "I charged it on your credit card. I hope you don't mind."

"Not at all," he murmured against her neck. When she gasped in surprise he smiled against her silken skin and raised his head reluctantly. Mischief danced in his eyes as his inquisitive fingers once again inspected the fastening. "Is this all that's holding this thing together?"

At her nod, his eyes lit up. "Interesting."

She grinned. "I thought you'd think so."

"Are you going to take this off and take a shower with me?"

"No."

He sighed. "I didn't think so. Maybe next time?"

At his woebegone face, she laughed in spite of herself and pushed him toward the stairs. "Maybe. Go cool off so we can eat dinner."

He left her with obvious reluctance, and Georgia turned and walked into the kitchen as if in a dream, her smile soft and womanly as she lit the candles on the table. At the touch of her hands the French doors opened onto the patio, letting in the night. The muted strains of jazz drifted in from Bourbon Street, a dark echo of the hunger that throbbed in her blood.

Suddenly she gasped and whirled to face the kitchen. The food! She had completely forgotten about it! She ran to the stove, but even as she lifted the lid on the jambalaya, she knew it was too late. It was a scorched, sticky mess, unfit for a dog. How could she possibly serve it to Wes?

Tears burned her eyes. The bisque and bread pudding would have to be enough. But then the acrid scent of burning food drifted from the oven, and with a cry of outrage, she flung open the oven door, gasping and coughing as smoke rolled into her lungs. How could she have forgotten to set the timer? The pudding looked like a crispy critter, and Georgia cursed it soundly as she tossed the mess into the garbage.

She heard a chuckle, and with a start, she whirled, the sheepish apology that sprang to her lips dying at the sight of her husband standing in the doorway. Could all that rugged masculinity really belong to her? she wondered as her eyes freely roamed his body. He was a magnificent specimen of a man, lean, tough, hard as granite when the mood suited him, but so very endearing when he chose to be.

He was dressed all in black, and if it wasn't for the appreciative laughter twinkling like stars in his black eyes, he would have looked like the devil himself. But no devil could smile like an angel and take her to heaven with a touch, a kiss. And the promise in his eyes was enough to make her forget almost everything but the two of them. She smiled tremulously.

Wes pushed himself away from the doorjamb and lazily closed the distance between them. "You're turning the air in here blue," he teased. "What's wrong?"

She blinked, confused. "What?"

"Why," he asked patiently, making no attempt to hold back his laughter, "are you cussing like a sailor?"

"Actually, there are three reasons." She pointed to the pot on the stove. "There's the first one. The second's in the trash, and the third's in the refrigerator." Humor came to her rescue, and her eyes were sparkling as they met his. "Put them all together and they spell dinner. Or disaster, depending on your point of view."

"Is that a hint that I'm not going to like dinner?" he asked cautiously, his lips twitching traitorously.

"No, that's an understatement. You're going to hate it." Suddenly depressed, she threw down the spoon. "Oh, Wes, I'm sorry!" she wailed. "I wanted tonight to be perfect, but it's awful. I burned the bread pudding, and the jambalaya's terrible, and I forgot to warm up the bisque. I feel like such a fool!"

"Honey, you're not a fool," he admonished gruffly as his arms closed around her, the laughter that threatened quickly buried under a wave of tenderness. "I'm sure it's not that bad. Come on, let's eat and you'll feel better."

"No, I won't. It's terrible."

"You're just being paranoid," he scoffed and filled his plate before she had time to protest further. "If you used Mark's recipe, you couldn't go wrong. Would you like me to serve you?"

She eyed the generous serving he had given himself and quickly snatched up her own plate. "No, thanks. I just want a little. Wes, this is silly," she protested again as she sat across from him at the candlelit table. "Believe me, you won't hurt my feelings by not eating this. Why don't we go get a hamburger or something?"

"No. I'm not sharing you with anyone tonight." Without another word, he took a bite of the jambalaya. And almost gagged. She hadn't been kidding when she'd said it was awful. But he'd have tried to eat mud pies if she'd made them. He swallowed bravely and forced a boyish grin. "I don't know what you were worried about, honey. This is . . . delicious."

Georgia heard his hesitation and watched him struggle through two more bites with foolish tears stinging her eyes. How had she ever had the good fortune to fall in love with such a crazy, wonderful man? She reached over to stop his hand as he carried the fork to his mouth for the fourth time, her eyes bright with a love she made no attempt to hide. "This isn't necessary, Wes."

"What?" he asked innocently. "I wish you'd eat, honey. This is great. I think I'll even have it for breakfast."

His utter seriousness was her undoing. She burst into laughter, and when he calmly took another bite, she held her stomach, convulsed by another fit of giggles. "Stop!" she cried weakly, tears sliding down her cheek. "You're going to make yourself sick."

He grinned and pushed back his plate, grabbing her hand before she could wipe away the tears. When he leaned over to do it for her, she held her breath, and his mouth lifted in a crooked grin. "Feeling better?"

She nodded, his unexpected gentleness creating a funny ache in her stomach. "You didn't have to take a chance on getting food poisoning just to cheer me up."

"It was worth it to see you smile." In one little movement, he came to his feet and tugged her up beside him. A dark swath of hair fell back from his forehead as he tilted his head back to inspect the night sky. When his eyes returned to hers, they were aglow with starlight. "Let's go for a ride," he urged. "It's a beautiful night to put the top down."

"But aren't you hungry? You haven't eaten anything decent."

"I don't want anything but you," he rasped huskily. "Are you coming or not?"

A shiver of awareness danced along her spine, and she knew that this was what she'd been waiting for, the chance to put herself unequivocally in his hands. There were no doubts, no hesitation. "Of course I'm coming. Dinner may have been a bust, but I've still got first claim on you tonight."

"Speaking of busts," he drawled, deliberately dropping his hungry eyes to her breasts, "don't you think you should wear a sweater or something? Not that I mind," he hastily assured her when she looked at him in surprise. "But I'm sure as hell going to mind if somebody else looks. If anybody ogles you, they're going to get punched out."

He meant it, she realized with a start of amazement. He would come to her defense without giving it a second thought, without asking, without caring if she were in the wrong. Three months ago she would have laughed at the very idea of accepting a man's protection when she was perfectly capable of taking care of herself. But now, it was nice. She squeezed his hand before slipping out of reach. "I'll get a shawl while you get the car."

The car was a vintage 190SL Mercedes, its red-and-chrome exterior babied and polished until it sparkled like the stars overhead.

They drove for what seemed like hours, sometimes

talking, sometimes enjoying a silence that was comfortable and easy. But always on the edge of consciousness was an aching awareness of each other that tugged at the senses and baffled the mind. The whispered movement of silk in the darkness teased and taunted until Wes thought he would go mad with the need to touch her.

At first the dark, empty streets and warehouses that surrounded them didn't register. Then Georgia saw the river and the huge freighters moored there. She frowned and sat up straighter. "Where are we going?"

"You'll see. Just be patient."

But patience wasn't one of her strong points, and when Wes parked the car and pulled her aboard an old steamboat tied up at the wharf, she was too alarmed to keep quiet. "Wes, what are you doing?" she hissed, vainly trying to tug free of his hold. "We can't just walk onto this boat like we own it! We're trespassing!"

"No, we're not." He laughed. "I *do* own it."

"You *own* a steamboat? *This* boat?" At his nod, her mouth fell open. The boat was huge, with three decks, cabins, and a magnificent paddle wheel at the stern. But even with the relatively few lights on board, she could see it was sadly in need of repair. She turned questioning eyes to his, but he once again pulled her after him like a wayward child. "Will you please wait a minute," she complained. "I want to look around."

But he never even looked back. "In a minute. I want you to meet someone first." When he reached the pool of light at the bottom of the stairs that led to the second deck, he stopped so suddenly she plowed into his back. "Sorry," he chuckled as he swiftly turned to steady her. "I forgot something." And with no more warning than the devilish gleam in his eyes, he deliberately pulled her lace shawl open and gazed hungrily at her breasts. Georgia felt the heat all the way to her toes. She needed, ached for the touch of his hands on her, and he didn't disappoint her. With agonizing slowness he reached out to slowly trace a pouting nipple that was clearly revealed by the clinging silk of her dress, searing her with his hot touch, teasing her until she thought she would die. Her knees melted, and a moaning protest escaped her throat when the caress was abruptly ended. "Wes, please—"

It took every ounce of control he had not to drag her into his arms. He wanted her more than he had ever wanted a woman in his life, and he was damn sure going to have her. Later. And with that litany spinning in his head, he once again reached for her shawl. This time he rearranged it so that she was primly covered. When his eyes lifted they were black with passion. "This is the last time you wear that dress out of the house," he said hoarsely. "It's indecent."

A smile played about her mouth. "I know. That's why I bought it."

"And it's worth every damn penny," he growled, giving her a quick, hard kiss before once again taking her hand. "Come on. I want you to meet Pierce."

Pierce Lawton, Georgia soon discovered, was the boat's pilot, guard, and general repair man. And what he didn't know about a steamboat wasn't worth knowing. He had the weathered face of a man who had spent his life on the river, with long brackets on each side of his mouth, crow's-feet at his eyes, and a year-round tan.

He was a man of few words. When Wes introduced her as his wife, he didn't bat an eye. "Welcome aboard, Mrs. Hayden."

"Thank you," she said softly. "And please call me Georgia." Her gaze was inexorably drawn to the graceful, shadowed lines of the boat. "This is the first time I've ever been on a steamboat. It's beautiful."

Wes grinned as his old friend's eyes lit up and a smile creased his face for the first time. Georgia couldn't have said anything that would have won Pierce's heart faster.

"*It* is a *she*," he stressed gruffly. "And she's just as stubborn and temperamental as a woman, too. She has to be handled gently."

"It's so dark," Georgia complained, her voice wistful. "I can't really *see* her the way I'd like to."

"Come back one day next week and I'll give you a tour."

Wes's dark brow shot up in surprise. "I thought you didn't give tours, Pierce," he teased.

The older man's glare was fierce. "I don't, but you've never had a wife before."

Wes laughed, not disturbed in the least by the crusty river man's huffiness. "Georgia's never seen New Orleans the right way . . . from the river. Let's show her."

The steamboat was soon moving downstream at a slow, lazy pace, and the city lay before them like a sparkling jewel, its lights brilliantly reflected in the languid water of the Mississippi. The breeze was cool off the water and only the splash of the paddle wheel disturbed the quiet of the night. Georgia couldn't help but wonder why anyone would choose a faster mode of travel when they could have this peacefulness. She sighed, and Wes immediately slipped his arm around her. "Tired?"

"Oh, no," she hastily assured him. "This is just so relaxing. Is that why you bought the boat? So you could get away from business and play Tom Sawyer?"

He smiled slightly, and even in the poor light, she could see his solemn eyes. He stared out over the dark water, suddenly far away. "When I was a kid," he said quietly, "I used to sit on the levee and watch the *Delta Queen* come in." Memories clouded his eyes. "She was the most beautiful thing I'd ever seen, and I never got tired of watching her. I even tried to sneak on board once. The captain caught me. He took me on a tour, and I knew then I was going to buy my own steamboat one day."

"And you have," she replied lightly, though his melancholy tugged at her heartstrings. How many times had he stood on the outside looking in, wanting what he couldn't have? This was one of the few times he'd let her see the hurt, the loneliness he must have suffered as a child, and she ached to console him. "She's a beautiful boat, Wes—"

"I'm going to have to sell her."

"Sell her!" she cried in confusion. "But you just said . . ."

"I know." He dragged his eyes away from the past and smiled sadly into her upturned face. "It's ironic, isn't it? I worked my tail off to get that boat, built Sam's Place into a success, and now I have to sell the boat because of the business."

"But the restaurant can't be doing that badly. It's always packed. And you're expanding!"

"And the boat needs a lot of repairs," he countered. "I can't afford to do both."

"But surely if you just wait," she protested. "I know you're going to need a lot of money for the new restaurant, but the boat means so much to you. Can't you do something?"

"Honey, don't get upset. I can get another boat," he assured her as he drew her into his arms. "It's not the end of the world."

"But there must be a way—"

"Hush," he growled huskily, gently closing her mouth with his.

Surprised by the rush of hunger that streaked through her, Georgia never thought to resist what she had been waiting for all evening. His kiss was slow and lazy, delicious, warming her blood like a brandy over a low flame, intoxicating her. Heat sprinted all the way to her fingertips, and with a murmur of pleasure, she crowded against him, seeking the fire that blazed just under his skin.

A groan tore at his lungs as the crests of her breasts hardened against his chest, burning him, driving him mad with wanting. He spread his legs to draw her closer, cradling her against his thighs, a sudden urgency thundering through him. He had to have her.

In one swift, decisive movement, he reached down to slip his arm beneath her knees and lifted her against his chest, never breaking the kiss, hungrily exploring the dark sweetness of her mouth.

Georgia gasped at her sudden weightlessness, struggling up through the passion that swamped her to wrench her mouth from his. "Wes? What about Pierce?"

His black eyes bored into hers. "I told Pierce that we're staying on board tonight. He won't disturb us," he said hoarsely. "I want to make love to you, but I've got to hear you say it's what you want, too. I need to hear the words, honey."

Was he as unsure of her as she was of him? she wondered in amazement. Her mind had fought with her heart at every turn, and even though he'd never said he loved her, it no longer mattered. She couldn't keep him at arm's length anymore, not when he was the one person in the world she couldn't live without.

"Yes," she answered simply. "I want you, too."

His arms tightened convulsively around her. "You little witch," he rasped thickly as he carried her toward the staterooms that opened directly onto the deck. "I thought you were going to say no again, and I couldn't stand the thought of another cold shower. Do you know how long I've waited for tonight?"

She laughed and looped her arms around his neck. "Two months, six days, and about seventeen hours."

"So you've been counting, too," he noted with a satisfied grin, and he pushed open the door to the stateroom with his shoulder.

It was a suite, actually, but Georgia only had time to gather scattered images before Wes was letting her legs go so she could slide down his body till her toes touched the floor. A sitting room and bedroom. The richness of mahogany. An ancient floral carpet and a living-room suite. And Wes. She leaned against him and fell into the warmth of his eyes. "Wes, this is beautiful. You can't sell it."

His hands dragged her close, letting her feel the passion that was just barely held in check. At the blush that stole into her cheeks, he grinned wickedly. "I didn't bring you in here to discuss the pros and cons of selling this boat," he said dryly.

Her green eyes widened innocently. "Oh? Then why did you bring me in here?"

"Because I want to do wonderful, wicked things to your gorgeous body," he growled, a rakish gleam in his eyes. "Any objections?"

"Not as long as I get to return the favor," she retorted promptly and pulled his head down to hers. At the taste of his mouth, the feel of his tongue sliding over hers, desire flashed like lightning, and the fires she thought were banked spread out of control. Her heart thundered wildly in her breast, stealing her breath, the ache in her loins sweet and painful.

Her soft, pliant body tore at his control. God, she was hot! Even through the cool silk of her dress, her heat called to him, enticing him. He had to touch her, feel her skin next to his. Blindly, his long, searching fingers groped at her waist, the seconds stretching into eternity before he found the damnable tie that had been torturing him all evening. He tugged, and her dress whispered to the floor like a falling rose petal. Her hose and lacy white panties soon followed.

"You're beautiful," he murmured, kissing the pulse that pounded in her throat. "Here. And here," he sighed against her breast, taking the rosy crest into his mouth, laving the sensitive peak with his tongue before gently closing his teeth around it. At her cry of delight, he smiled and moved lower. The smoothness of her skin was like silk under his mouth, his tongue. "And here," he rasped against the gentle swell of her abdomen.

"Wes, please," she cried in a voice rough with passion, pleading with him to continue his exquisite torture, to assuage the ache that throbbed deep inside her. Everywhere he touched fire raced along her skin, destroying her control, weakening her into a quivering mass of desire that threatened to melt at his feet.

His mouth traveled slowly back up to her waiting lips. "Please what?"

"Love me," she whispered, pulling at his shirt.

"I thought you'd never ask."

They explored each other with an ever growing urgency, their whispered sighs and muffled groans fanning the flames of a passion that hovered dangerously close to the edge of pain. His body tight with tension, he tasted the soft underside of her breast, lingered at her navel, nibbled at the tender inside of her thigh until desire pooled at her center like warm honey. She writhed helplessly, her hips arching into his, her lips seeking his as the flames of passion licked at her.

Suddenly, the need was too great, the desire too intense, and she guided him to her eagerly, pulling him into her warmth, her very soul. Her arms and legs surrounded him, holding him close as they raced to the stars together. His strength, his passion surged into her, sweeping her toward the edge of the universe, and with a startled cry, an almost unbearable tightness gripped her body and time seemed to stop. Her nails bit into the strong muscles of his back. "Wes!"

"I've got you, sweetheart," he growled deep in his throat. "It's okay. Let yourself go." And with one powerful thrust, she was free-falling through space, pulling him after her into a world of sensual delight.

Slowly, reluctantly, she floated back to earth in Wes's arms, her body totally relaxed, sated. She was too happy to move, warm with a contentment she'd never known before. If only the night would never end, and Wes would never leave her arms. "See what you've been missing by not coming home to dinner?" she teased sleepily.

His soft chuckle stirred the damp tendrils clinging to her temple. "Don't worry, honey, you made your point. From now on, I'll be home every night."

7

They returned to the house late the next morning, their arms wrapped around each other, touching, and stealing kisses at every opportunity. And the laughter that warmed their souls was shared, intimate, precious. The night had been wonderful, filled with loving, and Georgia hadn't wanted it to end. She wasn't ready to leave paradise or to test the fragile happiness they had found in the harsh realities of the real world. But when they stepped inside the house she discovered they had no choice. The phone was ringing. With a grimace, she picked it up, her arm slipping around Wes's waist as she leaned against him. He kissed the corner of her mouth, drawing a smile from her before she reluctantly turned her attention to the caller. "Hello?"

"Mrs. Hayden?" Sarah Gardner sobbed with relief.

"Thank God! I've been trying to reach Wes all night. Is he there?"

"Yes, of course," Georgia assured her and quickly handed the phone to Wes. "It's Sarah," she explained at his puzzled expression. "She sounds upset."

Wes frowned and jerked the receiver to his ear. Sarah Gardner was not a woman who rattled easily. "What's wrong, Sarah? Is there a problem at the restaurant?"

"No, it's Danny!" she cried. "He's in jail." And with that admission, she completely fell apart.

Wes cursed under his breath, his relief that the problem wasn't at the restaurant short-lived. Danny Gardner. He should have known. For the last few months he'd been making his mother's life a living hell, running with a rough crowd, coming in at all hours of the night, falling into one scrape after another. Sarah couldn't do a thing with him, and although Wes had tried reasoning with him, he'd known it was only a matter of time before the boy got into serious trouble. It was a hard way to learn, but getting arrested just might be the impetus he needed to straighten out his life before it was too late. "Calm down, Sarah, and tell me what he's being charged with."

"Malicious mischief," she said, sniffing indignantly. "Danny never did anything malicious in his life! I told that stupid desk sergeant that, but he still wouldn't release him. I've got to get him out of there, Wes!"

"Just sit tight," he advised calmly, "and let me see what I can do. I'll be in touch." When he hung up his face was grim. "Sarah's son, Danny, is in jail. For malicious mischief."

"What are you going to do?" Georgia asked quietly as he once again picked up the phone.

"Call my lawyer and try to get him out. And take a piece out of that kid's hide the next time I see him."

She promptly reached over and hung up the phone. "Have you forgotten there's a lawyer in the family now?"

Irritation snapped in his eyes. "Of course not! But Sarah's my employee, and it's my responsibility to handle this."

My employee, *my* responsibility. His words jabbed her in the stomach, warning her to back off. Stunned, she stepped away from his touch, her face suddenly pale. "In other words, you don't want my help."

"Damn it, honey, I didn't say that! It's just that I'd rather you didn't get involved with Danny Gardner. That kid's got a chip on his shoulder as big as the Rock of Gibraltar, and he won't take kindly to any overtures from you. He runs with a rough crowd, and I don't want to see you hurt."

"I don't bruise that easily," she argued, accepting his concern, but not his logic. She couldn't stand on the sidelines and watch him lead a double life, one with her and one without. That was her mother's mistake, but it wouldn't be hers. Their marriage would be a full partnership even if she had to fight him every step of the way. "I know you want to protect me, but can't you see how impossible that is for me? I can't sit on my hands when someone needs help. Wes, he's just a kid."

"He's fifteen going on fifty," he snapped. "And too damn smart for his own good. Stay out of this."

Her eyes narrowed dangerously. "Is that an order?"

"Maybe."

"Then maybe you'd better read our prenuptial agreement. I never agreed to *obey* anyone."

He glared at her, his lips thinned in an angry line, his hands clenched at his side. She had to be the stubbornest woman he'd ever met in his life! "All right, damn it! Have it your way. You will, anyway. But don't expect me to like it."

He stormed upstairs, and slowly, heavily, she followed. The honeymoon was definitely over.

They drove to the police station in a silence that was thick with disapproval and resentment. In spite of the humid heat that left her navy suit clinging to her back and shoulders, Georgia shivered, chilled to the bone. How could this have happened? her heart cried. Last night they were so close they'd touched each other's souls; now Wes sat only inches away, but it might as well have been miles. An apology trembled on her lips, but she caught it just in time, forcing it back. Why should she apologize? she thought indignantly. She was a lawyer, for God's sake! The big, bad world he was trying to shield her from wasn't new to her, and she didn't need him to protect her from it.

Within minutes of their arrival at the police station, Georgia discovered Danny was being held by the juvenile authorities, and she quickly saw to his release. But the paperwork took time, and as the moments passed, impatience gnawed at her. She was achingly aware of every tick of the clock, the beat of her heart, Wes's brooding countenance as he stood in the background, his arms crossed over his chest, looking formidable in a conservative black suit that emphasized the midnight sheen of his hair and the bottomless depths of his eyes.

When Danny was finally released Wes reluctantly made the introductions before leading the way to the car. But Georgia hardly noticed his continued stiffness, her thoughts in a whirl. Danny Gardner was not at all what she had expected. She had prepared herself for a brazen bully who would, no doubt, try to intimidate her, not this tall, lanky, quiet boy who somehow looked out of place in jeans and a black RUSH T-shirt. Almost painfully thin, with his black-rimmed glasses and conservatively cut brown hair, he had the face of a bookworm, a scholar. Granted, his blue eyes were sullen, resentful, in fact. But they also showed an intelligence that should have steered him clear of trouble. He should have been spending his time in the library instead of with a bunch of thugs that were hell-bent on their own destruction.

"Why don't you tell me what happened, Danny?" she suggested after they'd climbed into her Volvo and Wes had turned the car toward the French Quarter. "Then we can see about getting you out of this."

Danny stared out of the window, ignoring her, and anger sprang into Wes's eyes. "Danny!" he barked warningly, but Georgia leaned over to touch his knee, shaking her head almost imperceptibly.

"We don't have to discuss this now," she told Danny calmly. "But you're going to have to give me your version of what happened, you know. You have a hearing in two weeks, and if you're found guilty, you could find yourself in a foster home for juvenile delinquents. And I'm sure you don't want that." He still didn't answer, but she saw turbulent emotions flicker in his eyes and sighed in relief. He wasn't nearly as unmoved as he pretended. "I think we can prevent that, though. Come by the house tomorrow afternoon and we'll talk about it."

Grudgingly, he nodded.

Georgia waited only until they had dropped Danny

at Sarah's before asking Wes about a possible job for the boy. "Wes, that boy's got too much time on his hands. No wonder he's in trouble, with Sarah working late every evening and nothing to do at home. Can't you find him a job?"

His fingers bit into the steering wheel. "Don't start this, Georgia. You know I don't have any openings. And don't look at me like that."

She stiffened. "Like what?"

"Like I'm an unfeeling monster. Like I don't give a damn about that kid. I asked Danny months ago if he was interested in a summer job, and he turned me down flat. I couldn't very well force it on him."

"But, Wes, there must be something we can do. . . ."

"You can't help him if he won't help himself," he said flatly. "Believe me, honey, I know what I'm talking about. He has to make the first move."

"And what if it's the wrong one?" she demanded. "You may be able to sit back and wait for him to make a mistake, but I'm sorry, I can't. I've got to at least try to help him."

An angry flush burned his cheeks. "You don't think I've tried?" He whipped the car over to the curb as they reached the house, indignant anger knotting the muscles along his jaw as he turned to her. "I've talked till I'm blue in the face, trying to make him understand what he's doing to his life. I've even taken him fishing and hunting and everything else I could think of to try to knock that damn chip off his shoulder, but nothing works. Everything I say just goes in one ear and out the other."

Georgia could have bitten off her tongue for her hasty words. "Wes, I'm sorry. I didn't realize—"

"Why do you think I wanted you to stay out of this? I didn't want to see you beat your head against the same brick wall I've already come up against. But I should have known you wouldn't listen." His eyes pinned her to the seat. "Is the rest of your family as stubborn as you are?"

"It's a family curse," she replied with a weak smile.

He wasn't amused. "That's what I was afraid of." He reached across her to push open her door. "I've got to get back to work now. I have a few more building sites to check out, and I'll probably be home late, since I gave Sarah the night off."

"But—"

He gave her a swift, hard kiss, ignoring her objections as she reluctantly stepped from the car. "Try not to worry yourself sick about Danny. You'll only be wasting your time." And before she had time to do anything but step back from the curb, he was gone.

He didn't come home for dinner, and Georgia was miserable. When he still wasn't home at midnight, she climbed into their big, empty bed and tried not to miss him. But the clean, masculine scent of him clung to the sheets and surrounded her, and it seemed like hours before she finally slept.

She awoke in the morning to find that his side of the bed had been slept in, but she was alone. And it hurt. In spite of his dictate the previous afternoon, she did indeed worry herself sick, but not about Danny.

She hadn't given Danny a second thought since the previous afternoon. So when she opened the door to him shortly after lunch, she couldn't suppress a pang of guilt. Damn Wes for distracting her this way! He had no right to take her to the stars one night then drop her the next.

Danny took one look at her standing in the open doorway, and his indifference slipped. "Are you all right, Mrs. Hayden? You look kind of funny."

"Thanks," she said dryly and waved him inside. He was right, of course. She looked awful. She was pale, tired, and queasy, and not even the bright, red-and-white blouse and navy slacks she had pulled on could improve her spirits. Only Wes could do that. She cursed silently and ushered Danny into the living room. She would *not* let Wes jerk her emotions up and down like a yo-yo just because she loved him.

Danny perched on the edge of one of the blue camelback sofas, his uneasiness readily apparent from the uncomfortable flush that fired his cheeks and the way he nervously wiped his hands on his jeans. Georgia felt her spirits sink. Having him meet her at the house was a mistake. He'd never unbend enough to talk to her.

"Why don't we go for a drive?" she suggested with a smile. "I need some fresh air." And so it seemed, did he. He was at the door before she'd had time to grab her purse and keys.

For a while she drove aimlessly, not saying much, letting the wind whip the cobwebs from her brain and the nausea from her stomach. From the corner of her eyes, she watched Danny begin to relax, but he seemed perfectly content to let the silence between them continue. Georgia took a steadying breath and jumped in with both feet. "What happened the other night, Danny? What were you doing at that ware-house?"

He stiffened. "I wasn't doing anything," he mumbled defensively. "Just looking at the ships tied up at the docks."

"What about the boys you were with? They were caught spray-painting the side of that warehouse. Are you saying you didn't help them?"

"No."

"Then why did you run from the police?"

"What do you care?" he lashed out angrily, the youthful lines of his face hardening with suspicion and hurt. "No one else believed me. Why should you?"

"Because I don't have any reason not to," she answered simply. "And I can't help you if I don't know all the facts."

He laughed shortly, bitterly. "You want facts? You got 'em. I was somewhere I shouldn't have been, with some guys who don't give a damn about other people's property. And I knew what they were doing and I didn't try to stop them. I guess that makes me as guilty as them."

"Not necessarily," she argued. "Did you approve of what they were doing? Is that why you were with them?"

"No."

"Then why didn't you try to stop them?"

"Are you kidding?" he scoffed. "Those guys weigh over two hundred pounds each. They'd have demolished me."

"Whose idea was it to go down there?" When he told her it had been his, she frowned. "Why?"

"I told you. I wanted to look at the ships."

Why, Georgia wondered, had no one noticed where this boy's interest lay? Wes had claimed he was uncooperative and resentful, and maybe he was. But he was also troubled and without any male guidance in his life. There had to be a way to reach him. She turned toward the warehouse district. "I think you're going to come out of this all right, Danny."

"You do? Why?"

"Because you were an innocent bystander whose only mistake was choosing the wrong friends." Her eyes met his for just a second before she turned them back to her driving. "You're going to have to drop them, you know. But I think I can help you find some new ones."

She refused to tell him anything else, but when she pulled up in front of Wes's old steamboat, Danny's eyes widened. "God, she's beautiful," he breathed hoarsely. "Who owns her?"

Georgia grinned and switched off the ignition. "Wes. Come on, let's go aboard."

They found Pierce in the engine room, his face smudged with grease, dressed in coveralls that were patched with stains. He hastily wiped his dirty hands on a rag taken from his back pocket and advanced toward them, the solemn expression of his weathered face belying the twinkle of welcome in his eyes. "Back for your guided tour?"

"You didn't think I'd forget, did you?" Georgia teased, pulling Danny forward to make the introductions. She watched the two shake hands before explaining to Danny, "Pierce takes care of the boat for Wes. He's also the pilot, so if you've got any questions, he's the man to ask."

Pierce's shrewd eyes noted Danny's fascination with the engine room. "You like boats, son?" he asked suddenly.

Danny's eyes snapped back to his. "Yes, sir!"

"Well, what are you waiting for? Look around."

That was all the encouragement the teenager needed. When he had hurried away to inspect the repairs Pierce had been making, Georgia turned to the older man with a grateful smile. "I hope you don't mind my bringing him," she began.

"Have you forgotten your husband owns this boat?" he reminded her dryly. "Of course I don't mind." His narrowed eyes strayed back to Danny. "He's a quiet kid. He's in some kind of trouble, isn't he?"

There was no criticism, no condemnation in his voice, only concern. Encouraged, Georgia quickly explained the situation. "He needs something to get him back on the right track, Pierce, and he's crazy about boats. Could you use a helper?"

"I could use about ten of them," he replied promptly. "But Wes is going to sell the boat. I thought he told you."

"Oh, damn! I forgot!" she cried. "I was so sure I could help Danny, I completely forgot Wes was going to sell it. Pierce, we've got to do something. There must be a way Wes can keep the boat. It's his dream. He can't sell it."

"I agree. But right now he can't afford both, especially since the boat is only for his personal use. It's hard to justify keeping it when it doesn't bring in a penny in revenue."

"But if he could use it for some sort of commercial enterprise—" She stopped short, stunned by a sudden idea that sprang full-blown into her mind. She clutched at the older man's arm. "Pierce . . . the restaurant . . . why can't it be on the boat?"

He didn't, thank God, laugh at the idea. Georgia could practically see the wheels turning in his mind.

She held her breath, waiting for his opinion, and he didn't disappoint her. "I think," he said finally, "you may have hit on something. Come on, let's check it out."

Georgia and Danny caught up with him on the main deck, and for the next two hours they went over every square inch of the old steamboat. There was no question that there was more than enough room for the conversion. As Georgia explored the lounges and staterooms for the first time, she was thrilled with the craftsmanship of the boat. It had all the grace and beauty of the Old South, and with the right decorating, it would make a gorgeous restaurant.

She was riding high on a wave of optimism when she finally started back home. Everything was going to work out just fine. Danny hadn't been able to contain his enthusiasm for the boat; and when Pierce had offered to take him home later if he wanted to stay a few more hours, Danny had jumped at the chance. She smiled fondly as she thought of the older man. Pierce might be crusty and gruff, but he wouldn't steer Danny wrong, and that was what she was counting on. They would be good for each other.

And Wes would be ecstatic. Maybe now he would see that he didn't have to worry about her. She could take care of herself. Making a snap decision, she turned the car toward the restaurant.

Slipping past Sylvia, who, thankfully, was tied up on the phone, Georgia let herself into Wes's office, excitement turning her eyes to sparkling emerald chips. He was at his desk, and for just a minute she indulged herself and stared at him hungrily.

He looked tired, she realized, noting with concern his tousled hair, the weary set of his broad shoulders beneath his light blue shirt. His jacket had been discarded, his steel-blue tie loosened at the neck, and with a start, Georgia realized she'd never seen him looking quite so disheveled. Or solemn. She longed to take him in her arms and bring back the flashing smile that was so dear to her heart.

She started toward him only to stop in her tracks when he looked up suddenly. "Georgia! What are you doing here?"

"I wanted to see you. And since Muhammad wouldn't come to the mountain . . ."

"Sorry. I've been working on the plans for the new restaurant, and I lost track of time. I'll try to be home for dinner tonight."

"You're working too hard, you know," she warned him, and before he realized her intentions, she swiveled his chair until his back was to her. "Don't move," she growled and gently began to massage the back of his neck and shoulders.

Her touch was too sweet to resist, and with a groan Wes relaxed, leaving his body at her mercy. He couldn't have been in better hands. Small, feminine, and strong. She knew just where to touch him.

The feel of his strong shoulders beneath her hands tempted her to explore further, but he was tired. And she couldn't quite forget the way he'd been avoiding her for the last twenty-four hours. She wanted some answers, intended to have them, but later. Now she had to convince her husband he didn't have to give up his dreams. Her hands tightened on his shoulders. "I saw Danny today. And Pierce. And I may have come up with a way to kill two birds with one stone. With some help from you."

He frowned. "What are you talking about?"

Her fingers rubbed hypnotic circles on his temples. "Danny and your steamboat," she explained softly. "Danny loves it, and if you'd offer him a job helping Pierce, I know he wouldn't turn it down."

"And what about when I sell it?" Wes demanded, reaching up to capture her hands as he whirled to face her. "Have you thought of that? If he really became attached to the boat, that could be a real blow to him."

"But you don't have to sell it," she countered triumphantly. "Turn the boat into your new restaurant."

He stared at her as if she'd lost her mind. "How in the world did you come up with that idea?" he finally asked.

"Actually, it was a joint effort. Pierce and I worked it out, and it's a beautiful idea, Wes. We went over every inch of the boat, and it's perfect—"

"No."

She stared at him, stunned. "What do you mean, no?"

"No, it's a bad idea. Too complicated. Too risky. Just the structural changes alone would cost a fortune."

"Not that many changes would have to be made—"

"Damn it, Georgia," he snapped, "will you please let me take care of my own business!" First she'd worried about Danny, and now him. And that was the last thing in the world he wanted. She was pregnant, for God's sake! She should be relaxing and taking care of herself instead of worrying. And if she wouldn't watch out for her health, he'd have to do it for her. He came to his feet, his face grim. "I don't want you involved in this. I can handle it. Why can't you just be a wife and mother and trust me to take care of our finances? I can, you know."

The blood drained from her face. Of course he was worried about the baby. That was the only reason he'd married her. She'd been stupid to forget that, but she wouldn't do it again. Oh, no, she'd never do it again.

She stepped back, her chin held high. "You're right, of course. I'm sure you know what you're doing, and you certainly don't need my help. Sorry."

She turned and walked out, her whispered apology lingering to echo in his ears, her scent clinging to the air, the painful glint in her eyes stabbing him in the heart. "Damn!" he whispered fiercely as the door shut behind her retreating back. What the hell was wrong with him? All he wanted to do was protect her, but he was always saying the wrong thing, hurting her. Did she have any idea what her tears did to him?

8

Time dragged its feet the rest of the afternoon, and Wes found it almost impossible to concentrate on the site reports that lay on his desk before him. Every time he tried to visualize the parcels of land he'd spent the past few weeks investigating, he saw the steamboat instead. And Georgia. Always Georgia. He couldn't banish her from his thoughts; she was like a ray of sunshine in the cloudy corners of his mind, teasing and caressing him at the most unexpected times. When, he wondered in surprise, had she come to mean so much to him?

She'd slipped under his guard when he wasn't looking. Stubborn, willful, independent, she'd charged right into his heart, and he hadn't been able to lift a finger to stop her. He'd handled her all wrong. He laughed shortly. He'd been so determined to show her he was the boss, he hadn't realized he'd spent most of his days thinking of her, all of his nights dreaming of her.

His fingers closed around the site reports. She was right about the steamboat. He could never hope to build a restaurant that would compare with the style and beauty of the riverboat. But could it be converted into a restaurant? He reached for the plans.

When he let himself into the house an hour later he glanced ruefully at the roses he held in his hand before hiding them behind his back. He wouldn't blame her if she threw his peace offering back in his face if he gave her half a chance. He'd acted like a real jackass.

He came upon her unaware on the patio, her back to him as she kneeled to weed a flower bed that really didn't need it. A pair of faded cutoffs hugged the swell of her bottom. His body tightened with need, and for one fleeting moment he was tempted to lean over and kiss the tender skin of her nape, revealed by her upswept hair. He grinned, discarding the idea almost immediately. If she was still upset, she probably wouldn't hesitate to knock him out of his shoes.

Georgia stabbed at the dirt with a gardening tool, her thoughts in a turmoil, anger and hurt struggling for dominance. Damn Wesley Hayden! He had woven his spell around her, bewitching her, giving her false hope in a situation that was hopeless. The baby was the only reason for his concern for her, and if this afternoon had taught her anything, it was that he resented her intrusion into his life. Well, he could damn well rest easy. She wouldn't intrude again.

The sound of a footstep on the flagstone walkway scattered her thoughts, and she turned with a start. Wes stood less than three feet away, his tie hanging around his neck, his blue shirt unbuttoned, his dark eyes devouring her. She jumped to her feet, her eyes meeting his defiantly. "What are you doing home so early?"

"I told you I'd try to be home for dinner," he reminded her. "Anyway, I had some business to take care of, and I couldn't let it slide any longer." He pulled the flowers from behind his back and stepped toward her. "I'm sorry, honey," he said gruffly.

She stiffened on suddenly wobbly legs. "For what?"

"For acting like a jackass. For saying all the wrong things." Regret darkened his eyes. "I didn't mean to hurt you."

She took the roses reluctantly, avoiding his touch, forcing herself to ignore the warm rush of love that invaded her heart with his apology. Of course he wasn't intentionally trying to hurt her. She had never thought he was, and that was what made it so painful. He could devastate her without half trying. She turned blindly away, unwanted tears stinging her eyes. "It doesn't matter," she said huskily. "I shouldn't have interfered."

He winced. She was hurt worse than he'd thought. And she was already rebuilding the wall between them with mortar he himself had supplied. Damn it, he had to do something before she completely walled him out. He studied the graceful lines of her back, the strength in her slim shoulders, the pride in the way she carried herself, and knew he couldn't let her go. Not now. Not ever. She had come to mean too much to him. "After you left the office I started thinking about your suggestion about the boat," he told her with a nonchalance he was far from feeling. "I may have rejected it too quickly."

Georgia froze, her pulse skipping as his breath feathered the back of her neck, somehow breathing fire into her blood. She closed her eyes weakly. "May?" she choked.

"All right, I definitely rejected it too quickly," he admitted ruefully, his eyes alight with indulgence. "It's a good idea. I still have to take a look at the boat, but I think it'll work. And the renovations won't cost nearly as much . . . hey, wait! Where are you going?" He laughed in surprise as she grabbed his arm and whirled him toward the house.

"To the boat," she replied, grinning. "Before you have time to change your mind."

He insisted on changing into something more comfortable while Georgia impatiently cooled her heels in the entryway. By the time he appeared at the top of the stairs, dressed in jeans and a navy polo shirt, she was convinced he was dragging his feet just to tease her. "I'm going to have to get you some vitamins," she muttered when they were finally in the car.

"What was that, sweetheart? I didn't catch it."

"I said Grandma was slow, but she was old. What's your excuse?"

He chuckled and grabbed her hand, bringing it to his mouth to plant a lingering kiss on her palm. When her breath caught in her throat he smiled softly. "What's the hurry?"

Her hand tingled from his touch, and with just a push she would have fallen into the bottomless depths of his eyes. "I . . . I . . . it's g–going to be dark soon," she stuttered inanely.

"I know," he growled with a wicked grin. "I can't wait."

She laughed in spite of herself. "You're impossible. I meant—"

"I know what you meant," he interrupted. "And you know what I meant."

When they arrived at the boat Wes tied her to him by simply clasping her hand in his. When she looked at him in surprise he said, "Stay close, okay? I don't want to have to go looking for you when it gets dark."

She blushed. "I thought you wanted to look at the boat."

"I'd much rather look at you," he countered honestly. "You're much easier on the eye."

"But turning this boat into a restaurant will make it easier on your pocketbook. Come on."

Hand in hand, they wandered from room to room, deck to deck, and Georgia was hard pressed to contain her enthusiasm. After the episode in his office, though, she wasn't all that anxious to have her head bitten off again for giving her opinion. So she watched him inspect the lounges and staterooms and had to bite her tongue to keep the words from spilling out. It's his boat and his restaurant, she reminded herself. Let him make up his own mind.

"What do you think?"

She blinked, dragging her attention back from her thoughts. "What?"

"What do you think of having the dining room in here?" he repeated patiently. "Do you think this lounge is too small?"

"I don't know," she said evasively. "Whatever you think . . ."

Wes swore silently and reached out to grab her chin, forcing her to look him in the eye. "Honey, if I didn't want your opinion, I wouldn't ask for it. Now, what do you think?''

Her eyes searched his, but she couldn't doubt his sincerity. She sighed, suddenly lighthearted, and turned once again to examine the lounge. "I like the idea of having several small dining rooms," she finally replied. "On a slow night you can use just one of the rooms, so it won't look quite so empty. In the winter, you'd only have to heat the rooms you're using, and it would be a lot more intimate . . . as long as you don't crowd a lot of tables into it." She clasped his arm eagerly. "Oh, Wes, can't you see it? Once the boat's restored to its original condition, it'll be beautiful! It's just crying out for gas lamps and white-coated waiters. And red carpet! You'd have to have live entertainment —jazz, of course—and you could even cruise up and down the river, and rent the boat for private parties, and . . ."

"Whoa, whoa," he laughed, pulling her to him to give her a quick hug. "You're going too fast, honey. I admit that sounds great, but there are a few problems you haven't thought of. Like where we're going to tie up. Right now we're not exactly in the best part of town, you know. And what kind of clientele are you aiming for? So far it sounds pretty expensive."

"No more expensive than Sam's Place," she assured him. "Anyway, you won't have any problem with that as long as the prices aren't completely out of sight. The boat's the main attraction, and once it's renovated you won't be able to keep the people away from it."

His narrowed eyes ran thoughtfully around the lounge, repairing with his imagination the scarred mahogany and worn carpet, filling the room with music and flowers and happy customers. When his gaze returned to Georgia he grinned and slipped his arm around her waist to pull her close. "You know something, Mrs. Hayden? I think you're right."

"Well, that's a switch," she teased, her eyes sparkling. "I thought I wasn't good for anything but staying home and having babies."

"Who gave you that idea? I can think of a lot of things you're good for," he replied suggestively. "Just stay out of the kitchen."

"Ohh! You—"

"Don't say it," he warned, then swooped down to take her mouth in a hard, searing kiss. For one timeless second surprise held her motionless, but then liquid heat curled into her stomach as his tongue explored the dark moistness of her mouth, and Georgia knew she was lost. With a murmur of pleasure, she collapsed against him, her arms twining about the strong column of his neck as she gave herself up to the delicious flames that licked at her.

With a groan, Wes deepened the kiss, a sudden rush of need firing his blood. His hands roamed wildly over her back, her hips, her breasts, touching, caressing, loving, finally cupping the sweet fullness of her buttocks to drag her close to the heat of his passion. God, she felt right in his arms, so soft, so feminine, so unbelievably passionate. Her heat scorched him, and he loved it. Her soft whimpers of need enflamed him, and with a ragged moan, he gave up all thought except that he needed her.

The sharp cry of a tugboat whistle ripped through the soft murmurs of their loving.

Georgia stiffened, suddenly remembering where they were. She dragged her mouth free and stared at her husband with eyes that were clouded with desire. "Wes . . . I . . . we shouldn't . . ."

"I know," he said huskily, his grin rueful, pained. "I didn't mean for things to get out of hand. It's just that you're so damn kissable."

"I am?"

"Quit fishing," he chuckled, once again taking her hand. "You know damn well you are. But if you want proof, you'll have to wait till we get home."

"Promises, promises," she sighed, her eyes dancing with mischief.

"You're pushing your luck, lady," he growled. "Come on, let's go home."

They stopped to pick up Chinese food, but once they reached the house their minds were hardly on dinner as they sat at the kitchen table and gazed into each other's eyes like a couple of love-struck teenagers. Wes captured her hand and pressed a kiss to it. His eyes were serious as they met hers. "You were right about putting the restaurant on the boat. I'm going to start the remodeling as soon as possible."

Tears burned her eyes. "I didn't want you to sell it."

"Hey, don't cry about it," he said in surprise. "Come here." And with a simple tug, he pulled her from her chair, around the table, and onto his lap. His arms closed around her with reassuring strength. "That's better. I don't like it when you're so far away."

He bent his head, his eyes darkening to black pools of desire, and brushed her lips with his. Heat flared. Back and forth, he repeated the caress, lazily moving over and around her trembling mouth with a teasing lightness that was as sweet and gentle as a baby's breath. A shuddering sigh escaped her parted lips, and

Wes drank it thirstily, the hot flick of his tongue joining the play, tempting her, enticing her to taste the dark desire he offered. With a moan, she melted over him like warm honey.

A delicious lassitude weighted her limbs, the teasing touch of his mouth driving out of the world. Need. She needed the pressure of his mouth on hers, his tongue mating with hers, his arms binding her to him for all time. "Wes, please," she moaned, "stop teasing me."

"I'm not," he denied huskily before delicately sinking his teeth into her lower lip. "Don't you want me to kiss you?"

"Yes! But this isn't—"

His waiting mouth eagerly swallowed the rest of her words, his tongue surging between her teeth, stealing her breath, demanding a response she was more than willing to give. She gave him her heart, and he took it, molding her to him, his hands possessive yet gentle as they ran down her back and circled her waist before tenderly cupping her breasts.

The pressure building within her tightened exquisitely, and with a gasp, Georgia pushed herself half-way out of his arms and grabbed at his shirt before he even realized her intentions. "Honey, wait!" he laughed as she pulled it over his head. "You're going to knock me out of the chair if you're not careful."

"Serves you right," she replied in a voice husky with laughter and passion. Holding his shirt between her thumb and forefinger, she deliberately dropped it on the floor before bringing her twinkling eyes back to his. "You started this. I'm going to finish it. Get out of those pants."

"Yes, ma'am," he drawled, his black eyes dancing,

and stood her on her feet before stripping off the remainder of his clothes. When he saw her eyes riveted on him, he quickly closed the distance between them and lifted her chin. "You, Mrs. Hayden," he told her with a broad grin, "are a wanton. A delicious one, but still a wanton."

Georgia blushed and kissed his naked shoulder as her arms snaked around his waist. "Would you believe I wasn't like this until I met you?"

"I sincerely hope not," he rasped and reached for the snap of her jeans. "Okay, woman, out of those clothes."

His hands were there to help, his fingers there to soothe, to tease, to tempt, stoking the flames that burned within her until the roar of the fire echoed in her ears, and she forgot everything but the man who held her in his arms.

"Come on," he growled against her lips, "let's go upstairs."

She looped her arms around his neck and nipped at an earlobe. "What's the matter? Too hot for you?"

Her tongue teased his ear, and for just a second he faltered, desire tearing through his body, threatening the fragile hold he had on his control. With a quick turn of his head, he captured her mouth in a punishing kiss that promised heavenly delights.

"Do you have any idea what you're doing to me?" he rasped thickly.

She smiled against his shoulder. "Mm-hmm. Want me to stop?"

He pushed open the door to their bedroom with his shoulder. "Don't you dare."

The sheets were smooth beneath her back as he

laid her gently on the bed, and with a sigh of pleasure, she pulled him down on top of her, her arms closing about him to hold him close to her pounding heart. She shuddered. "Wes, please . . . I can't . . ."

"Easy, sweetheart," he murmured, and surged into her, taking her with him on a wild ride toward the heavens. They left the world behind, need met need, desire met passion, drawing them ever closer to the edge of paradise. They reached it together, rushing into the darkness that consumed them as the earth fell away and reality became the feel of skin on skin, their breaths mingling, hearts beating as one.

Weightless, sated, Georgia drifted past the stars and felt their magic, a small, contented smile playing about her mouth. "I never want to move again," she murmured in dazed delight.

Wes laughed softly against her breast and rolled with her in his arms until she was sprawled across him. His black eyes glinted in the darkness. "You're not falling asleep on me already, are you? I'll just have to see what I can do to wake you up."

His fingers probed at her ribs, and with a gurgle of laughter, she squirmed against him. "Stop!" she laughed. "I'm awake."

"Just make sure you stay that way. You can sleep later. I want to talk to you."

She reached up to brush his lips with hers. "So talk," she said softly. "I'm not going anywhere." And she wasn't. A warm tide of love enveloped her, and she had to bite back the words that trembled on her lips. She wanted to tell him how much he meant to her, but she couldn't quite let go of the words. He'd never said he loved her, never hinted that he wanted her to love him. If it wasn't what he wanted to hear, would he turn away? She couldn't chance it. Not after what they had just shared.

He settled her more comfortably against him, his arm hooked around her waist possessively as he absently stroked her silky skin. "Just wait till we get the boat finished, honey," he sighed against her hair. "It's going to be great. We'll take moonlight cruises and have midnight suppers and make love till the sun comes up."

It sounded heavenly, and for tonight she couldn't deny herself the luxury of dreaming. She snuggled against him, her sigh of contentment caressing his chest. "Don't forget the champagne breakfasts," she reminded him. "And satin sheets. There's something so decadent about satin sheets."

"Anything you want, honey." He brought her mouth to his to give her a slow, sweet kiss. "Did I thank you for coming up with a way to save the boat for me?"

"You don't have to," she answered simply. "I couldn't let you sell it. It means too much to you."

"God knows why," he laughed. "Especially in its present condition. But it won't be that way much longer." A tug on her hair brought her eyes up to his. "I want you to stay away from there once the remodeling begins. There's no use taking any chances."

Uneasiness stirred in her stomach. "Wes—"

"Don't argue with me about this, Georgia. I mean it. I don't want anything to happen to you or the baby. Can't you understand that?"

Only too well, she thought dully. The baby, his

concern was all for the baby. Why did she have such a hard time remembering that?

He frowned at her sudden stillness, surprised that she didn't argue with him. "As soon as the structural changes are made you can go back. I promise. Okay?"

She nodded, unable to force the words through her tight throat. What did it matter? He didn't love her; he probably never would. She had to quit wishing for something she couldn't have. She was having his baby; that would have to be enough.

"I want you to do all the decorating," he continued. "You can hire anyone you want, including Danny. Just don't overdo it."

"No . . . I won't," she said thickly and squeezed her eyes tight against the pain that beat at her. His baby was all she'd ever have of him. Did he actually think she'd take a chance on losing it?

Her breath caught on a tiny sob, shattering the quiet of the bedroom. Wes jumped as if he'd been shot. "Honey, what is it?" he exclaimed in concern. "Did I hurt you? What's the matter?"

She buried her face against his throat, sudden tears scalding her throat, her arms clinging to his neck. "It's n–nothing," she choked.

"You don't cry over nothing," he said stubbornly. "What is it?"

What could she possibly tell him? she thought tearfully. That she'd been stupid enough to fall in love with him? She fought for control, but her voice was hoarse with the strain when she finally said haltingly, "It's just . . . the baby. This is an emotional time . . ."

"Are you sure that's all it is?" he asked doubtfully,

cradling her close. "I'm worried about you. You should see about getting a doctor."

Her heart constricted painfully. "Y—yes, I will. I'll try and get an appointment next week." But Wes still wasn't satisfied. Damn, he wished he knew more about pregnant women! She was always so strong, so controlled. Her tears completely unnerved him. He didn't know what to do, what to say, and he couldn't shake the suspicion that she wasn't telling him everything. Why? What was she trying to hide?

9

Georgia watched the kind brown eyes of the doctor as he examined her and couldn't quite shake the uneasiness that crawled into her stomach. It wasn't anything Dr. Landon had said; he was a relatively quiet man, with a calm, reassuring manner that seemed generally unflappable. And although his face was faintly lined, it was from the passage of time rather than worry. His expression was enigmatic, but his hands were steady, dependable. With his bushy white brows and thick thatch of white hair, he had the age and experience that instilled confidence. But somehow Georgia felt that she had surprised him.

She waited anxiously for him to finish his examination, but when he listened to her heartbeat and the baby's one last time, a sudden, inexplicable fear sickened her. "Dr. Landon, is something wrong?"

He smiled reassuringly and dropped his stethoscope

to his chest. "No, you're as healthy as a horse. Who was your doctor in Baton Rouge?"

"Dr. Fisher," she replied with a frown. "He's been our family doctor for years. Why?"

"And he's the one you went to when you suspected you were pregnant?" he persisted, ignoring her question.

"Well . . . no." She hadn't been able to bring herself to face the family friend who had seen her through measles and puberty. Not until she was sure. "I went to a clinic."

He reached for a pad and pencil. "What clinic? And what was the name of the doctor you saw?"

"I didn't see a doctor," she explained in growing confusion. "I just went in for a pregnancy test. When I called later for the results, the nurse told me it was positive. Dr. Landon, what's going on? Why are you asking me all these questions?"

He hesitated, searching for the right words. "There's nothing wrong with you, Mrs. Hayden," he finally said quietly. "But you're not pregnant."

He was kidding. He had to be kidding! she thought wildly. But there was no laughter in his eyes, only concern. She clutched at the edge of the examining table as ice invaded the deepest corners of her heart. *You're not pregnant, not pregnant.* The words beat at her, taunted her. The doctor was wrong. He had to be!

She grabbed at his sleeve, her green eyes wide with shock, her face ashen. "The test was positive. Don't you understand? I have to be pregnant. Why else would I have missed my period for three months? Why would I have morning sickness?"

And why, she silently cried, *would Wes have married me?*

He patted her hand consolingly. "I'm sorry, my dear, but all your symptoms point to a false pregnancy. There is no baby."

She couldn't doubt him; he was so firm, so *sure.* Dear God, what was she going to do now? An icy numbness seeped through her veins, chilling her to her very soul, and she was suddenly terribly empty, lost. The baby had only been a dream, a figment of her imagination, a mistake. It was all a terrible mistake. She slipped from the examining table and reached for her clothes with fingers that refused to stop shaking. "I have to get out of here," she said hollowly. "To think . . ."

"Why don't you let me call your husband?" Dr. Landon suggested, his craggy brows knit in a frown. "You've had a shock—"

"No!" Didn't he realize Wes was the last person she wanted to see? At this point just the sound of his voice would be enough to send her over the edge. "I . . . I can't see Wes right now. Please don't call him, Dr. Landon. I need some time to myself."

She could see he wanted to argue, but she was determined, and with a sigh of defeat, he gave in. "All right. But I want you to be careful driving home. You've had a shock, and your reflexes aren't what they should be."

"I will," she assured him huskily. "I'll go straight home."

Later, she didn't even remember pulling on her yellow-and-white knit dress or driving home. Her tortured eyes were riveted on the image of Wes when she had told him she was pregnant. No declaration of love, no promises of happily-ever-after, had been given, and none had been expected. He had insisted on marriage for the sake of his child. Nothing more, nothing less. And now the sole reason for their marriage no longer existed. It had never existed, and somehow she was going to have to find the words, the strength, to tell him.

Would he regret the loss at all? Would he feel the emptiness, the aching loneliness, that tore at her? Or would he only think she had engineered the whole story to trap him into marriage? He had to know she would never stoop to such deceit. He was the one who had pressured her, insisted on marriage despite all her arguments. He was the one who had wanted the baby to have the Hayden name.

Once she got home Georgia collapsed onto the couch in the living room. She had to face it. Once Wes learned there was no baby he would want a divorce.

What was she going to do?

Panic pulled her to her feet and dragged her back and forth in a restless pacing, and she found it impossible to think. In desperation, she reached for the phone and prayed Kurt would be home. He would be able to help her, he would know what to do. But at the sound of his voice on the line she was shocked by a lump of emotion that nearly strangled her. She took a deep breath, trying for a lightness she was far from feeling. When she finally spoke her voice was thick with tears. "Hi. Are you busy?"

"No, of course not. What's wrong? Did you and Wes have a fight?"

"Not yet."

"Does that mean you're planning one?" He laughed in surprise.

"No . . . I don't know. Oh, Kurt, what am I going to do? I'm not pregnant."

"What do you mean you're not pregnant?" His voice was hoarse with concern. "Did you have a miscarriage? Where are you? I'll be there as soon as I can."

"No! You don't need to come. I'm at home and I'm all right." She slipped down to the floor and rested her head against the couch, cradling the receiver to her ear. "There was no miscarriage. I never was pregnant. I went to the doctor today and he confirmed it."

"But . . . damn it, Georgia, how could you think . . ."

"It was easy," she cried. "What was I supposed to think when I had a positive pregnancy test?"

"How the hell did that happen?"

She sighed. "I don't know. There must have been a mix-up. Dr. Landon is checking into it for me. But what difference does it make now? It won't change anything." Her fingers gripped the receiver in growing panic. "How am I going to tell Wes, Kurt? How can I tell him it was all a mistake and he didn't have to marry me after all?"

"He's not a monster, Georgia," Kurt reasoned. "And it's not as if you planned this. He'll understand."

"He's going to be furious. I doubt that he'll ever trust me again."

She could almost see her brother's fierce frown. "If he gives you any hassles about this, you just let me know. I'll straighten him out."

"With brute strength, if nothing else," she teased weakly, his unfailing support a balm to her tortured spirit. "Thanks for the offer, but I don't think you'd be able to get through to him any better than I can. Once he gets an idea in his head he doesn't let go of it easily."

"But, sis, if he loves you, he's got to know you wouldn't deliberately fake a pregnancy just to get his ring on your finger."

"But he doesn't love me."

The silence at the other end of the line was full of shock. "You must be blind!" he finally exclaimed. "The man's crazy about you. Remember, I've seen the two of you together, and he could hardly keep his eyes off you. Or his hands, either."

"It was all an act, Kurt. For you and Dad."

"No one's that good an actor. Don't you want him to love you?"

"More than anything," she whispered. "But he doesn't want to love me. He only married me because of the baby."

Kurt snorted in disgust. "That may be what he said, but he didn't have to marry you. No one held a shotgun to his head. Did you pressure him to marry you?"

"Of course not," she said indignantly. "You know I'd never do that. I didn't want to get married."

His laughter was soft, triumphant. "My point exactly. He wanted to marry you."

"Only because he wanted the baby to be legitimate," she replied. "He's illegitimate himself, Kurt. He would never want his child to go through what he did."

"I can understand that. I'd feel the same way. But I don't think you're giving Wes a fair shake here, sis. Talk to him; give him a chance," he urged. "He just might surprise you."

She doubted it, but she wasn't in the mood to argue. "I hope so, but I'm not holding my breath." When she finally hung up, after promising him she would call him if she needed him, she looked at the clock and felt her heart drop to her toes. Time was running out; Wes would be home soon. She groaned. She couldn't just *sit* here. She reached for her keys and an escape she knew was only temporary.

Georgia drove for hours, aimlessly moving with the traffic, trying not to think, to feel. And, to a large extent, she succeeded. It was a gray day, with threatening storm clouds hanging low over the city. It matched her mood exactly. When it started to pour she hardly noticed. She automatically switched on the windshield wipers and rolled up the windows, but her mind was a blank.

The tears came, however, when she somehow ended up at the river and saw the steamboat tied up before her. It sat in the rain like a lost cat, huddled against the dock, looking unwanted and unloved, and not even the light shining from Pierce's cabin could dispel its gloominess. In the two weeks since Wes had decided to use it for the restaurant little had been done to the exterior. It was still weathered and gray from lack of paint, and it looked as tired as she felt.

Rain lashed at the windshield when she turned off the ignition, drumming out a hollow rhythm that echoed the painful pounding of her heart. In the lonely, gray world that surrounded her, she could no longer ignore the agony that beat at her from all sides. The graceful old lines of the steamboat softened and blurred as a torrent of tears engulfed her.

Great, wrenching sobs shook her slender frame, burning her throat, her eyes. And she, who hated to cry, cried as she had not done since her mother had died. She cried for the baby she had never really had, for the emptiness deep inside her, for the loss of a dream that had been so incredibly real, so precious. She cried for a love that wasn't returned, for a man who wanted her body and nothing else, for a marriage that had happened for all the wrong reasons. And, last of all, she cried for herself and the loneliness of the years that stretched before her.

It ended as quickly as it had begun, with the last tear sliding down a splotchy cheek and her breath catching on a sob. She was spent, and it was with only the greatest effort that she was able to lift her hand and wipe her eyes. She noted without surprise that the bleak, gray day had given way to an equally gloomy twilight, and it would soon be dark. She should have been home hours ago, but she couldn't find the strength to care. Nothing really mattered anymore.

The headlights of an approaching car bounced off the rain-splattered pavement to strike her in the eyes, but Georgia was too miserable to notice. When the slamming of a car door ripped through the quiet of the rain, however, and angry footsteps approached, she suddenly realized she was alone on the nearly dark wharf. Her stomach clenched with fear, she turned to face the danger only to go limp at the sight of Wes striding toward her. He jerked open the car door and slid in beside her.

"What the hell do you think you're doing?"

His angry bellow ricocheted off the windows of the car like striking hail, enveloping her in a maelstrom of fury Georgia knew she was in no shape to face. Her heart was too full of pain, her control too fragile. She edged closer to the door, her trembling fingers clutching the steering wheel. "Wes, you're all wet. You're going to ruin the upholstery."

"Do you think I give a damn!" he thundered. "Of

course I'm wet. I came home early to take you out to dinner, only you weren't there. When the storm came up and you still weren't home, I got worried. I've turned this town upside-down looking for you! What are you doing here?"

Her eyes skidded from his to look out at the rain. "I'm not doing anything, just looking at the boat."

"In the rain?"

"I . . . I needed some time to think."

"Damn it, Georgia! What the hell is going on?"

"Nothing!" she cried, pulling against the hands that held her. She couldn't tell him, not like this, when he was so furious. "Let go!"

"Not until I get some answers," he muttered, reaching up to switch on the dome light. His long fingers captured her chin, dragging her face up to the light, but at the sight of her red-rimmed eyes and blotchy cheeks, he paled, the air leaving his lungs in a rush. "Honey, what is it?" he demanded hoarsely. "Why have you been crying?"

His concern was almost her undoing. "I went to the doctor," she told him shakily. "Wes . . . the baby . . ."

His fingers bit into her shoulders. "What is it? What's wrong? Tell me, honey. Let me help you."

"Oh, Wes, there is no baby!"

Her anguished cry stabbed him in the heart. Dear God, she'd lost the baby! He reached for her, lifting her out of the bucket seat and onto his lap. "Oh, baby, I'm sorry, so sorry," he whispered against her hair as his arms wrapped her close, desperately trying to ease her hurt while his own body shook with pain. "You should have called me. What happened? Are you okay?"

Oh, no! her heart cried in horror. He'd misunderstood. He thought she'd had a miscarriage! She was in his arms under false pretenses and she couldn't stand it. She had to set him straight. She pulled back, trembling with fear. "Wes . . . there never was a baby. It was a mistake."

She could almost feel his body freezing beneath her. A mistake? What the hell did that mean? He grabbed her, suspicion turning his blood to ice water. "Are you trying to tell me you never were pregnant?"

"Yes," she choked, paralyzed by the sight of his grim, accusing face. He was so cold, so *controlled*, and she knew with a sinking heart that this was going to be much worse than she'd ever expected. She could already see him slipping away from her, hiding behind the hard, remote eyes of a stranger. Panic seized her. "Wes, please give me a chance to explain," she pleaded. "It's not what you're thinking."

He impaled her with a gaze that was pure ice. "And how the hell would you know what I'm thinking?"

"It's written all over your face," she cried. "You think I lied from the very beginning, but I didn't! I had a positive pregnancy test, Wes. What was I supposed to think? I had no reason to suspect there might be a mix-up at the lab."

His expression didn't change by so much as the flicker of an eyelash. "And what about the physical signs? Surely you're not so naive you can't tell if you're pregnant or not."

"Of course not," she snapped, stung. "It was a false pregnancy, with morning sickness and the whole bit. I didn't fake throwing up, Wes."

"No, but nerves can do funny things to a person.

It's nice to know you had some qualms about tricking a man into marriage."

"You were the one who pushed for marriage," she reminded him icily. "I had no reason to trick you when a husband was the last thing I wanted."

"Isn't that convenient now that you have my ring on your finger?"

She blanched. "That's hitting below the belt."

The reproach in her wounded eyes was like a knife twisting in his heart, and he wanted to cut out his tongue for hurting her. "You're right," he said huskily. "I shouldn't have said that." And without warning, he deposited her back in her seat. "I need some time to think, to sort this out. Can you drive home by yourself?"

"Of course, but where are you going?"

He reached for the door handle. "Nowhere in particular. I'll be home later."

"Be careful," she whispered, but the slamming of the door cut her off.

Instinct eventually carried her home and upstairs into the bathroom. For a long time she stood under the shower, thinking. She knew she'd only been fooling herself by thinking she had come to mean something to Wes. If he loved her, he wouldn't have doubted her so easily. He would have realized she was just as much a victim as he was.

There was no hope for their marriage if he felt she'd been lying all along. And she'd tell him so just as soon as he came home.

With trembling fingers Georgia grabbed a towel and dried herself before pulling on a lacy black nightgown. Back in the bedroom she stretched out on the bed to wait.

The night was unending, with only the echo of her heartbeat in her ears to break the silence that surrounded her. She yawned, her eyelids growing heavy despite her best efforts to stay awake. She could not go to sleep! she told herself fiercely, but she was tired in both mind and body, and she didn't stand a chance.

When the bedroom door crashed back against the wall she jumped up in alarm.

Wes looked like something swept in by the storm, dark, mysterious, mesmerizing. The midnight sheen of his hair was tousled and damp, falling over his forehead at a rakish angle that was infinitely appealing. Georgia's nails curled into her palms as she tried to ignore his wicked grin and the possessive light in his black eyes as they boldly inspected every inch of her revealed by the lacy nightgown.

He lounged against the doorjamb, his arms folded across his chest, a leer upon his handsome face. "Ah, sweetheart, I see you've been waiting for me."

Her heart lurched crazily before righting itself. "Wes, we have to talk."

"Not tonight we don't." Lazily pushing himself from the doorway, he sauntered toward her. "I can think of much better things to do than talk."

The purposeful glint in his eyes was all she needed to galvanize her into action. She scampered from the bed, her arms wrapped protectively across her breasts, her eyes wary as she watched him approach on legs that weren't the least bit steady. "You're drunk!" she accused.

"You're damn right. I had to drown my sorrows in order to think. It didn't work." He opened his arms wide, his black eyes compelling. "Come here, honey, and kiss me good night."

Her eyes fell on the clock. "You mean good morning. In case you hadn't noticed, it's six o'clock."

"Whatever," he shrugged. "But I still want that kiss." And before she could even begin to guess his intentions, he lunged at her.

"Wes . . . damn you, let go! Don't!" she gasped, outraged as his hands treasured the slinky smoothness of her nightgown with devastating ease. She struggled, pushing and shoving, her muttered curses ringing in his ears, but he only laughed, and somehow they landed on the bed in a tangled heap, his weight pressing her into the mattress, her nightgown trapped around her thighs. Fury leaped into her green eyes. "Have you lost your mind? Let go—"

"Don't fuss," he growled sleepily, nuzzling the side of her neck as he settled himself more comfortably against her, blissfully unaware of how his whiskers scraped her tender skin. "You're my wife even if you did trick me. . . . I should get something out of this."

What the hell was that supposed to mean? she wondered indignantly, just barely resisting the urge to throttle him. He didn't believe her, but he expected her to continue to make love with him even though he obviously thought her a liar. He was crazy! She did have some pride, even if she was so in love with him she couldn't see straight. She'd rather end their relationship here and now than let him use her. She wedged her hands between their bodies and futilely tried to push him off her. When he didn't budge her temper snapped. "Wes? Get off! I can't breathe."

His only answer was a low, rumbling snore that shook the bedroom walls.

10

~∞∞∞∞∞∞∞∞~

For one hysterical moment she wanted to laugh. But instead she gave in to a cry of hopelessness, of bitterness, of pain. He had found the ultimate way to strike back at her, and he didn't even realize it. He had simply chosen not to believe her, and nothing she could say, nothing she could do, would change his mind. Trust had to come from the heart.

The sense of defeat was devastating. He didn't know her at all if he could believe her capable of such deceit. He might have held her in his arms and taken her halfway to the stars, but it obviously hadn't meant a thing to him. And like a stupid fool she had entrusted him with her heart and soul. All she had gotten in return was suspicion, anger, and lust.

She slid off the bed, and headed for the bathroom. An hour later she made her way downstairs, the sweet fragrance of early morning assaulting her senses as she opened the doors to the patio and stepped outside. The freshness of the new day surrounded her, all signs of yesterday's storm gone, except for the few puddles that clung to the flagstone path and the unseen bruises on her ragged heart. She was, thankfully, once more in control of herself and her wayward emotions, and she meant to stay that way. An ice-blue silk blouse sighed with every breath she took, but despite its obvious femininity and the fact that it contrasted beautifully with her white slacks, she had chosen it because it contributed significantly to the mood she wanted to present when she had her next encounter with Wes. Cool, sophisticated, untouchable. She wasn't going to melt at his feet, and the sooner he realized that, the better. Her heart was once again protected by barriers that were impregnable, and she had no intention of letting Wes get close to her again until they straightened out the mess they had made of their lives.

The rising heat and humidity eventually drove her back inside, but by that time the serenity of the patio had already started to pall. She didn't need quiet, she needed action! And this interminable waiting was driving her bananas! The slow, insistent tick of the mantel clock was worse than the Chinese water torture on her already tattered nerves, wearing away at her. She found herself listening for the faintest sounds of life, the fall of a masculine footstep upstairs, the running of the water in the bathroom, but only silence echoed in her ears. And with each passing hour, her impatience increased tenfold until she thought she would scream. By the time the clock struck twelve, she knew she couldn't take any more. If he hadn't had enough sleep by now, it was his own damn fault. He should have come home at a decent hour.

She jumped up from the couch and turned toward the stairs only to run full tilt into Wes's arms. She gasped as the overriding force of his masculinity surrounded her, the sight of his bare chest and the jeans riding low on his hips driving all thought from her head. "Wes . . . I didn't hear you. I thought you were asleep."

"You thought wrong," he growled roughly, closing his fingers around her upper arms to keep her in front of him. She had no right to look so damn beautiful when he felt like something the cat had dragged in. He scowled, trying not to notice the way her blouse clung to her breasts. "I want to talk to you. *Now.*"

Her green eyes glinted warningly at his tone, her smile saccharine. "I'm surprised you still can. After all the alcohol you consumed last night, I thought you might have pickled your tongue."

"Don't get cute. I'm not in the mood."

"Oh, really? Well, that's too bad because I am."

She had to admit he was trying to hang on to his temper. He gritted his teeth on a cutting retort, the muscles in his jaws rippling with the effort, and abruptly released her. "I said talk," he replied tightly, "not fight. Do you think you can quit taking potshots at me long enough to have a civilized discussion?"

She flushed. "I'm sorry. You're right, of course." She stepped away and forced her face into an expressionless mask as she seated herself on the sofa. She watched him gingerly settle across from her and couldn't help the stirring of her sympathies. He was miserable. "Would you like some coffee? It might help your head."

He grimaced. "No thanks. I don't think my stomach would tolerate it." His eyes captured hers, all pretense of pleasantness falling away to reveal the grimness underneath. "Why'd you do it, Georgia? You knew it wouldn't work. Or did you think you'd get pregnant right away and I'd never have to know?"

The suddenness of the attack stunned her. With an inarticulate cry, she bounded to her feet, her eyes blazing. "How dare you!" she hissed. "I didn't come to you begging you to marry me. I wasn't so desperate that I had to trick you."

He surged to his feet and glowered down at her. "Oh, I'll admit you were very clever about it. You let me talk you into it. You wanted marriage right from the beginning; you can't deny it. And when I didn't fall for your sexual blackmail, you resorted to this little scheme. Why don't you just admit it and be done with it?"

"Because it's not true!" she snapped, seething. "*You* were the one who had to get married, not I." She advanced until she was just inches from him. "You wouldn't listen, damn you!" she cried, jabbing him in the chest with her finger. "You never listen! You're only interested in your point of view, and to hell with the rest of the world. Well, believe it or not, you're not the only one trapped in a marriage you didn't want."

She was too angry to see the flicker of surprise in his eyes, too hurt to note his sudden stillness, his doubts. He grabbed her finger. "Georgia—"

"Don't!" She couldn't stand his touching her, not when he thought she was a liar and a cheat. "Don't touch me," she whispered painfully. "It isn't necessary."

Frustration tore at him. Was she telling him the truth? Had she really had a false pregnancy? Her tears were real enough, but asking him to believe there was a mix-up in the lab was going too far. Damn it, what the hell was he supposed to believe? He had to get to the bottom of this.

But the ringing of the doorbell cut him off before he even opened his mouth, and the moment was lost.

Georgia welcomed the intrusion with a heartfelt sigh of relief. She'd had enough pain in the last twenty-four hours to last her a lifetime; she couldn't take any more. She hurried to the door, tears welling in her eyes at the sight of a grinning Danny and Pierce standing on the front steps. She pulled them inside, a tremulous smile flickering around her mouth. "What are you two river rats doing this far from the water?"

"Looking for you," Danny replied promptly, his blue eyes alight with an excitement he could hardly contain. "Pierce is going to start teaching me to pilot the boat. Want to come along?"

Wes stepped into the entryway, a frown darkening his brow. "Are you ready for that?"

"I'll have my hands on the wheel at all times," Pierce assured him quietly. His watchful eyes bounded between Georgia's pale face and the impatience clearly visible in his friend's eyes before he turned his attention back to Danny. "I don't think this is a good time for Georgia. We'll ask her some other time."

"But, Pierce, you said she probably needed to get out of the house . . ."

"I do," Georgia said quickly, shooting the older man a grateful look. "Just give me a few seconds to change into my jeans and I'll be ready." Without looking at Wes's suddenly tense figure, she turned and ran up the stairs.

She knew she was acting like a coward, using Danny and Pierce to run out on Wes, but she couldn't help herself. His contempt was strangling her.

With trembling fingers, she shed her sophisticated clothes and pulled on jeans and a blue-and-white striped tank top. She was tying her tennis shoes when Wes strode purposefully into their bedroom, his face unsmiling, determined.

"We're not through with this discussion, Georgia."

"Maybe you're not, but I am. There's nothing left to say."

"The hell there isn't," he snapped. "It may not be what you want to hear, but you're going to listen whether you like it or not."

Her eyes narrowed dangerously. "Not now I'm not because I'm going with Pierce and Danny. I'll be back later."

"Don't you dare walk out on me!"

She shut the door on his angry bellow and ran down the stairs, the smile she flashed the two men waiting for her never reaching her eyes. "Come on, let's go."

Little was said on the way to the boat, and Georgia was thankful neither of her companions commented on her silence. She doubted if Danny even noticed, he was so excited about taking the boat out. She smiled as her eyes fell on the teenager. He had been spending long hours with Pierce over the past month, learning as much as he could about the steamboat and the ways of the river, and he didn't seem to care that he hadn't seen his troublemaking friends in weeks.

Because of his reformed behavior since the incident at the warehouse, Georgia had persuaded the juvenile authorities to give him a chance by dropping the charges against him. He was back on the right path, and with each passing day he became more open and happier. Georgia found it hard to believe he was the same boy who had once sullenly refused to talk to her.

"Are you coming up to the pilothouse with us?" he asked as they arrived at the boat.

She smiled faintly and shook her head. "No, you two go ahead. I'll stand at the bow."

When he looked as if he might argue, Pierce intervened. "Are you going to stand here and jabber all day or help me cast off?" he teased. "I can't do it by myself."

"I'm ready when you are," Danny said, saluting smartly, his eyes twinkling brightly from behind the lenses of his glasses.

"Then get going. Time's a wasting." He watched him hurry off before turning to Georgia, his expression unusually sober. "Can you stick around for a while when we get back? I'd like to talk to you for a few minutes if you have the time."

"Of course," she said in surprise. "Is this about Danny?"

His face became even grimmer. "No . . . Wes. I'll see you later."

After he hurried off to help Danny, Georgia slowly made her way to the bow, no longer able to hide her misery. Wes didn't want to believe her because he obviously wanted out of their hasty marriage. Why else would he accuse her of plotting such an idiotic scheme? Didn't he realize that if she'd really tricked him into marriage, she would have claimed a miscarriage instead of baldly admitting she'd never been pregnant?

The city skyline passed in a blur off the starboard bow, but it could have been the Taj Mahal for all Georgia saw of it. Her dreams were falling all around her, and she didn't even notice when Pierce turned the boat around and headed back upriver. It wasn't until he appeared before her a few minutes later that she realized the boat was once again at its mooring, its engines still. She blinked, as if suddenly coming out of a daze, and hastily summoned a weak smile. "That was quick. How did Danny do?"

"Just fine. But if it'd been left up to him, we'd be halfway to St. Louis by now. I convinced him you wouldn't want to leave Wes."

Her smile fell away. "I may not have a choice in the matter."

A craggy brow quirked in surprise. "Problems already?"

"There've been problems from the beginning." She looked out over the muddy Mississippi. "I shouldn't be talking about this to you. You're his best friend."

"Does that mean you can't trust me to keep this conversation to myself?"

"Of course not!" Startled, she whirled to face him. "That's not it at all. I just don't want to put you in the middle."

His teeth flashed in a rueful grin. "You're not. I'm on your side."

"But you don't even know what we argued about."

"True, but I know you're the best thing that's ever happened to him."

"I don't think he'd agree with you," she replied dryly. "Right now he thinks I trapped him into marriage."

"I hope you don't believe that. Wes is too streetwise to get trapped into anything. He married you because he wanted to."

God, she wanted to believe that, but she couldn't. She'd seen the contempt in his eyes. "That's not what he says, Pierce. He's furious."

"That's just his wounded pride talking. You've got him in a tailspin, and he's running scared."

"Wes? Scared?" She'd never even considered it. He always seemed so sure of himself, so positive. "But why?"

"Because he's had damn little love in his life," the older man admitted gruffly. "He doesn't know how to handle it." He patted her shoulder awkwardly. "Give him a little time, Georgia. He's worth it."

Her eyes were sad as they met his. "I'd probably wait forever if he'd just trust me. But I don't think that's going to happen." Depression threatened at that thought, but she hastily shook it off by slipping her arm through his and giving him a wobbly smile. "I heard you've really been busy with the renovations. Can I see?"

"Of course. Come on."

She quickly realized that viewing the repairs was a mistake. The lounge on the lower deck was in a state of upheaval. Its worn carpet had been taken up to reveal the naked wood underneath. The oak paneling was being stripped of the white paint someone had foolishly used to cover the natural beauty of the wood. But in her mind's eye Georgia saw the plans she and Wes had made for the restaurant taking shape. The new red carpet would bring out the burgundy color in the priceless Tiffany stained-glass windows that looked out over the bow of the boat, giving the lounge a warmth and brightness that would make the customers' wait for a table in the dining room much more enjoyable. Intricately scrolled latticework decorated the Grand Staircase that rose gracefully to the next deck, and overhead, a delicate crystal chandelier needed only to be cleaned and repaired to elegantly light the way. The customers would never know that the boat hadn't always been this way or that the partitions that enclosed the kitchen and dining areas were painstakingly constructed to match the steamboat's original design.

When it was finished it was going to be spectacular. But she probably wouldn't be there to see it. If Wes continued to doubt her, there was absolutely nothing to keep her in New Orleans.

The lights along the river were just beginning to twinkle when Pierce dropped her at the house before taking Danny home. He didn't say anything in front of the teenager, but the look he gave her encouraged her to take heart. And for a few fleeting moments she did. He was right. Wes would never have gone into a marriage he didn't want, regardless of the circumstances. But somehow that thought slipped from her mind when Pierce's car disappeared around the corner and she was left to face Wes alone. She hesitated, her fingers trembling on the doorknob, silently cursing her shaking knees. She had nothing to be afraid of. Wes would never hurt her, and anything was better than not knowing where she stood. With a defiant toss of her head, she charged in.

He stood in the wide archway that opened onto the

living room, glowering at her. "I was just going to look for you. After the way you ran out of here, I wasn't sure you'd come back."

Somewhere in the back of her mind, she noted the way his white knit shirt emphasized the lean, powerful lines of his chest and shoulders, but her gaze was riveted to his face. His eyes were as cold and empty as space, without a spark of warmth or affection, and she knew with an aching sense of loss that she had once again been relegated to the rank of an outsider. He was shutting her out as effectively as if he'd shoved her out the door. "I didn't *run* out," she said quietly. "We both needed some time to cool off. Do you still think I lied to you? Because if you do," she continued before he could open his mouth, "I can give you the name of the clinic I went to in Baton Rouge. You can call and get the results of the pregnancy test for yourself. If you won't believe me, then maybe you'll believe a total stranger."

"That's not necessary," he replied tightly, inwardly wincing at the pain and anger shadowing her eyes. "It won't change anything. You're not pregnant and we're already married. You need to decide what you want to do."

Fear clutched her heart. "What do you mean?"

"Do you want a divorce?"

"Do you?"

He hesitated. That was the last thing he wanted but he wasn't going to put any more pressure on her. If she stayed, it had to be because she wanted to. "The decision is yours," he finally said quietly, "but I don't think you should rush into anything, especially a divorce. After all, we're already married. The damage is done."

Pained laughter ripped through her. "That certainly lets me know where I stand."

"Damn it, Georgia, I didn't mean it that way!" he ground out through clenched teeth. "Quit taking everything I say so literally."

"Then say what you mean," she replied huskily. She stepped toward him, not caring that her heart was in her eyes. "I can't read your mind. If you want to try and make our marriage work, you've got to tell me, Wes. What do you want?"

"You," he rasped thickly and eliminated the distance between them in two long strides. With infinite gentleness, he reached out to caress the curve of her cheek, running his fingers down the petal softness of her skin to her jaw, stealing her breath as her blood thundered through her veins. He could feel the trembling that gripped her, the wariness that tied her in knots. Soothingly, his thumb caressed the trembling lines of her mouth. "I've always wanted you," he said softly. "Didn't you know?"

She struggled for words, but her voice had deserted her, and she could only nod dumbly, unable to tear her eyes from his. How easily he destroyed her defenses. With just a touch, her bones melted, her thoughts scattered with the wind. Her heart tripped and fell, leaving her caught in a sensuous trap from which there was no escape.

Wes saw the conflict that raged within her, the doubts. She was hurting, and somehow he had to ease her pain. Slowly, carefully, he framed her face with his hands and waited for her to reject him. When she didn't, he lowered his head to hers. His lips touched hers with the softness of a feather, gliding over her mouth like a sigh, hesitantly testing her response with the faintest pressure, asking for nothing more than she was prepared to give.

With a husky growl, Wes deepened the kiss, possessively taking control of her mouth, one hand tangling in her hair while the other slid to the base of her spine to urge her closer. He drank from her lips greedily, drawing her very soul from her. His heart knocked against hers in perfect rhythm, the feel of her hips moving against his driving him wild. He wrenched his mouth from hers and covered her face with short, impatient kisses, his breath as ragged as hers. "Let's forget about yesterday, honey," he whispered hoarsely into her ear. At her delicate shudder, fire shot into his loins, and he pulled her closer. "This is what's important, what we have together. Nothing else."

"No," she murmured, struggling against the hot undertow that threatened to drag away her reason. She pushed him away, and pain rushed in. "No! I can't forget it. I can't pretend yesterday never happened."

"Georgia, honey, it's over and done with," he argued persuasively, reaching for her. "We're married, and all the talking in the world won't change that. Isn't that the important thing?"

"Not if you feel you were tricked into it. Not if you really don't want to be married to me." She avoided his touch, hugging herself, suddenly chilled by doubts. "How do you feel about me, Wes? About our marriage? Can't you see I have to know!"

She could almost see the shutters dropping into place. "You know I want you," he replied stiffly. "And I don't want to lose you. But I can't say what you want to hear. I don't know if I love you."

She winced, unprepared for his honesty. "I can't

remain in this limbo indefinitely," she said in a strained voice, "never knowing where I stand with you, not even knowing if we've got a chance at a future together. You've got to make up your mind. If we're going to make this marriage work, you've got to accept me totally. I won't be your wife just in bed."

11

What the hell are you talking about?'' he growled, irritation furrowing his forehead until his dark brows almost met over the bridge of his nose. ''You're my wife. Morally, legally, and every other way that matters. You sleep in my bed, eat the food I provide for you, and have complete control of this house. What more do you want?''

''You,'' she replied simply. ''All of you, not just the nights. I can't be happy walking two steps behind you, waiting for you to remember my existence.'' She saw the wariness creep into his eyes and wanted to give him a good, hard shake. Why did he have to be so defensive with her? Was she that much of a threat to him? She sank onto the couch and pulled him down beside her. ''Sit down, Wes. We might as well straighten this out right now.''

''What?''

"What you expect of me as your wife. You want me to cook and clean and look after your needs. Right?"

"Is that asking too much?"

She smiled wryly, without apology. "It is of me. You know I'm not cut out to be a housewife. A housekeeper can take care of this house much better than I can. Cleaning bores me, and I'm a lousy cook. Even you have to admit that."

A reluctant grin pulled at his mouth. "Your intentions were good."

"You can't eat intentions." Her fingers tightened on his arm. "I didn't marry the house, Wes, I married you. I won't be your servant, but if you'd just let me, I could contribute to our marriage in other ways. Then I wouldn't feel so useless."

The easy laughter that had sprung up between them vanished. "How?" he asked suspiciously.

"By working with you." Her eyes turned to the simple, elegant lines of the living room, the blue and green decor that blended so beautifully with the tropical greenery of the patio, before coming back to the man seated next to her. "I love the house, but I need something more to occupy my time, my mind. David held a position for me. I can always go back to Baton Rouge."

"No!"

She jumped, her heart pounding in alarm as her eyes flew back to his. "What do you mean, *no*? I told you I had to find something to do."

"You have plenty to do around here," he reminded her curtly. He'd be damned if he'd let her walk away so easily. "You promised to decorate the boat. And I'd also like you to arrange a party for the grand opening.

I'll be too busy to do it myself, and I know I can trust you to do it right. Will you do it?"

How could she possibly accept? she thought wildly. She was crazy to even consider it. She couldn't stay married to a man who didn't love her, who resented her presence in his life. All her instincts urged her to run while she had the chance, to get out before he destroyed her as her father had destroyed her mother. But Wes had found a way for her to stay when he could easily have let her leave. How could she turn her back on him after that? She nodded. "Yes, of course I'll do it."

Two weeks later she wondered what had possessed her to ever accept his offer. She had naively thought that he had found a way for them to spend more time together, but in reality she seldom saw him except in passing. Whenever she was at the boat, he was at the restaurant; and on those too frequent occasions when she just missed him, she couldn't help wondering if he was once again avoiding her. But then she would convince herself it was just coincidence, and she couldn't blame him if they were always interrupted by business. He was distracted, but then so was she. Suddenly there weren't enough hours in the day.

To say that she was busy was an understatement of the grossest proportions. She spent hours of each day scouring the city for antiques, hunting for just the right sideboards, the perfect highboys, always haggling with dealers over the prices. She visited dozens of carpet warehouses in search of a design that would match the original as closely as possible, but even then she had to go to Baton Rouge to find one. Wes left the choice of wallpaper up to her, as well as the linen, china, and flower arrangements, and the choices she had to make were incredibly difficult. When she could find the time, she was in the restaurant kitchen with Mark Reynolds, discussing the guest list for the party, the decorations, and always the food. Mark made countless dishes for her to sample, and after what seemed like weeks of taste-testing, they finally agreed on everything from soup to nuts.

Georgia was pushing herself. Doing double work, running around town like a chicken with its head cut off, wearing herself out until she was ready to drop. It was so much easier this way. She didn't have time to think, to feel, and when she fell into bed at night she was too exhausted to worry about the empty place beside her. He would be home eventually, of that she had no doubt. But that was all she was really sure of. Wes never mentioned their relationship, never acknowledged her need to know how he felt about her, but it was always there between them when their eyes met. She wouldn't wait forever.

But when he woke one morning with her in his arms, the only thought in his head was that it had been too long since he'd held her, too long since he'd kissed her. Her body was trusting in sleep, her cheek cushioned against his shoulder, the feel of her breasts crushed against his chest sweet torture. His hands wandered over her back in gentle exploration, dipping to her small waist, the flare of her hips, without conscious thought seeking and finding the hem of her black nightgown. The silky softness of her thighs tempted him to wake her, but not yet.

Once again his arms closed around her, and slowly, as if she were made of glass, he carefully shifted her to her back. She was exquisite in the morning light, the golden strands of her hair in beautiful disarray upon the pillow, her lashes dark fans against her pale cheeks, her skin alabaster against the midnight darkness of her gown. He frowned at the paleness of her skin, lightly tracing the edge of her gown from her shoulders to the soft swell of her breasts. The summer was half over, and she only had the whisper of a tan. He shouldn't have asked her to arrange the party. She was working too hard, and she was too damn thin! He could almost see her ribs! His palm flattened at her waist and slid to a halt at the curve of her breast, the slow, steady beat of her heart an unconscious caress against his hand. With an agonized groan, he leaned over and gently took her mouth, his body suddenly heavy with desire.

Georgia floated awake on a cloud of feeling, only gradually realizing that the sensuous dream that warmed her blood was all too real. Her body tingled, alive with a sweet tide of emotions that flowed through her like molten gold, weighting her limbs with a delicious lassitude she had no desire to fight. She smiled as her arms stole around the man she loved, her murmured good morning swallowed by his tender kiss. His hand captured a breast, his knowing fingers touching, teasing, urging the sensitive peak to a burgeoning hardness. She sighed and arched into him, hungry for more.

Wes tore his mouth from hers and leaned down to capture a nipple in his teeth, tugging ever so gently before lovingly laving it with his tongue. Heat curled into her stomach, wrenching a moan from her, and his own body throbbed in response. He dragged her close and buried his lips against her neck. "Do you know how much I've missed kissing you awake?" he growled in a voice thick with passion.

She cuddled against him. "You make a wonderful alarm clock. Do you have a snooze button?"

"Is that a hint that you want to go back to sleep?" he demanded with mock sternness. "Too bad, lady. I've got you at my mercy."

Her arms suddenly tightened around him. "You've always had me at your mercy," she admitted huskily. "Why do you think I kicked you out of my bed that first time? I'd stupidly fallen in love with you, and all you wanted was an affair."

"I still want an affair," he countered quietly. "With my wife. Is that too much to ask?"

She stiffened, ice invading her heart. "It is if that's all you're interested in," she retorted. Before he had a chance to stop her she scrambled out of bed and snatched on her robe, turning to face him defiantly. "I can't be happy with just a physical relationship. How many times do I have to tell you that? I won't settle for half a loaf."

He rolled from the bed with an angry growl, unconcerned with his nakedness. "Damn it, Georgia! Are you going to start harping about that again? Why can't you just accept what we have together and be happy?"

"Because we don't have anything!" she cried. With an angry exclamation, she grabbed his robe and threw it at him. "Would you please get dressed! I'd rather have this discussion in the living room."

"Tough!" he snapped, tossing the robe aside. "This time you're not calling all the shots." He stalked toward her, a glare darkening his brow. "You were happy when you thought you were pregnant. Is that the problem? You want a baby?"

"No!" How could he be so dense?

"Don't you want my baby? You did before."

She stepped back, alarm choking her as he drew closer. "You stay where you are, Wesley Hayden! I'm not going to discuss babies with you when you're stark naked!"

"You don't need to be afraid of me, honey," he coaxed, inching toward her. "You know I won't hurt you."

Tears welled in her eyes. "There are different ways of hurting," she said softly. "You tried to treat me the same way my father treated my mother, and I won't stand for it." Impatiently she wiped the tears from her eyes. "I wasn't happy when I thought I was pregnant, I was resigned. But you were too wrapped up in your work to notice. As long as I was in your bed at night, you didn't care how miserable or lonely I was during the day."

"That's not true!" he thundered, suddenly furious. "How could I know you were unhappy? You never said anything."

"I tried, but you wouldn't listen. What was I supposed to do? Leave you just to get your attention?"

"Isn't that what you're going to do anyway? You've been looking for an excuse ever since you found out you weren't pregnant."

She gasped, stunned. "You can't actually believe that?" But the answer was there in his eyes. The blood drained from her face. "I don't need an excuse to leave, Wes. There's no baby to tie me to you now; I could have walked out two weeks ago. Can't you see that I don't want to? I love you. I want this marriage to work."

His face hardened into unreadable lines. "But?"

"But I can't accept anything less than your love."

"Why is it so important for you to hear the words?" he demanded irritably. "Don't you realize I could just be saying them to keep you here?"

"No," she whispered, her heart in her eyes, "when you tell me you love me you'll mean it."

She was right about that. He'd never told any woman he loved her, had never even considered it. Until now. He swore silently and turned away to shrug into his robe, his movements quick and sharp as he belted it around his waist. He felt as if she'd slipped a choke collar around his neck, cutting off his air, his freedom. He didn't like it one damn bit. If he ever got the chance, he was going to tell Marcus Dupree just exactly what he thought of him. *He* was the one responsible for her fears, her insecurities. Any other woman would be thrilled to hear her man tell her she was beautiful and desirable. But not Georgia. No, she had to have all of him. Damn it, he wasn't a puppet on a string. He wouldn't perform on command.

He jammed his clenched fists in his pockets, frustration tying him in knots. When would she realize he was nothing like her father? He wasn't a skirt chaser; since he'd met her he hadn't even looked at another woman. How could he when she was all he thought of?

He sighed, suddenly very tired. "Can you give me some time? Maybe until the party?" he asked quietly. "I have to be honest with you. I've never been interested in making a commitment to anyone. And you're not just asking for love. You're asking for a lifetime. That scares the hell out of me."

She nodded. "I know, and I'm sorry. I'm not trying to put pressure on you, but we can't continue like this much longer."

"This isn't easy for me," he cautioned her. "I'm not sure I can give you what you want."

Don't say that! her heart cried, but she bit back the words, smiling sadly. "Give us a chance, Wes. Please."

"I'll try," he promised, and started toward the bathroom, only to stop and turn back to her. In one smooth, unhurried motion, he took her in his arms and pressed a long, lingering kiss on her parted lips. When he finally released her, he smiled into her wide, startled eyes. "Never doubt that I want you," he said huskily. "Nothing will ever change that."

But in the days that followed, she couldn't help but doubt him. He wasn't fit to live with; irritable and cantankerous, he lost patience with everyone, especially her. He avoided her at every turn, but when they did inadvertently stumble upon each other, his impatience and foul temper made her want to strangle him. She tried to find the humor in the situation—he was acting like a spoiled brat—but it was hard to laugh when he was always snapping at her. And when he moved out of their bedroom she saw nothing funny about it.

At first she thought he had just slept at the office. But when she woke close to dawn the second morning and once again found his side of the bed undisturbed panic set in. She hurried toward the stairs, intending to go down to see if his car was in the garage, when she heard muffled snoring coming from the guest room. She cautiously pushed open the door only to freeze. Wes lay sprawled on his back in the middle of the bed, the sheet negligently pulled across his naked hips, his arms flung wide.

Shock held her motionless in the doorway, but as realization penetrated the confusion in her mind, a slow, burning anger sparked, then spread like wildfire, consuming her. How dare he move out of their bed! she raged silently. Was this his way of telling her he had made a decision? He could at least have had the decency to tell her to her face.

She stomped over to the edge of the bed and shoved at his shoulder. "Wes! Wake up!"

He didn't even budge.

If she'd had a glass of ice water, she would have gladly thrown it on him. For days now she had hung onto her patience by a mere thread, but this was too much. She grabbed his shoulder with both hands and tried to jostle him awake. "Damn it, Wes! I'm talking to you! Wake up, you big . . . What are you doing?" she cried. "Let go!"

But it was too late. His arms had whipped around her with lightning speed, catching her off balance, tumbling her against the rock-hard wall of his chest.

Muttering dire curses, she struggled against the twin bands that held her, pushing against his bare chest with both hands, straining away from him. "Let go of me this instant!"

His only response was to tighten his arms around her waist, arching her hips against him. One dark eye opened to glare at her malevolently. "What the hell do you think you're doing?"

"I could ask the same of you," she hissed, punching him in the shoulder with her balled fist in a futile attempt to ignore the strength of his hard, masculine body pressed so intimately against her softness. "Why are you sleeping in here? Is there something wrong with our bed?"

He groaned and dropped his head back on the pillow. "You woke me up at the crack of dawn for *that*?"

Her conscience twinged at his tired sigh, but the anger that still held her within its talons refused to release her. "I want some answers, Wes. Why have you moved out of our bedroom?"

"Because I can't think with you pressed up against me," he snapped, goaded by her persistence. "And I refuse to let your sweet body tempt me into making a decision we might both regret. Okay? Am I making myself clear?"

"As glass," she replied icily. "May I get up now? Before I tempt you further and you completely lose your head? Heaven forbid that should happen—"

"Shut up," he muttered harshly and pulled her mouth down to his.

His kiss was hard. Georgia could feel the struggle going on within him, and its fierceness tore her apart. He didn't want to hold her, to kiss her, but she had

170

pushed him. And that was the last thing she wanted. He had to come to her willingly or not at all. Slowly, hesitantly, she backed out of the embrace, and he made no attempt to stop her.

"I'm sorry," she sighed. "I shouldn't have goaded you."

"I shouldn't have let you." His eyes were bleak as they met hers. "We've both been under a lot of pressure lately; and I don't know about you, but I'm exhausted. It's better if we don't have a physical relationship right now. I don't want to cloud the issues."

Better for whom? she wanted to cry, but she only nodded dumbly and slipped from the bed. "You're right," she said hollowly. "Whatever decision you make about us, I don't want you to have any reservations or regrets. I'll try not to bother you again."

The tension between them increased tenfold as the work on the riverboat neared completion. Wes worked like a man possessed, catching only four or five hours of sleep a night, but even those were haunted by the green-eyed beauty who tortured his defenseless body through his dreams. He couldn't shake her image from his mind even though he saw less of her than ever. Since their talk in the guest room she had taken to avoiding him, and he couldn't really blame her. Whenever she was near he couldn't help striking out at her in frustration. He ached for her, but he couldn't touch her. Once he did, he'd be lost.

The day of the party dawned fair and bright, a perfect summer's day. But Wes, viewing it through bleary, resentful eyes, couldn't appreciate the gorgeous weather. Today he opened his new restaurant, without having to sell the steamboat. He should be celebrating, but he couldn't summon any enthusiasm. Almost angrily, he stomped into the bathroom for a shower.

It was all her fault, of course, he thought in disgust as he emerged into the hall half an hour later, moisture still clinging to his hair and a navy towel wrapped around his lean hips. How could he let one five-foot-three slip of a woman tie him in knots this way? Where was his pride? She was no different from any of the other women who had come and gone in his life. Oh, she was beautiful. And intelligent. And he couldn't deny that every time he looked at her he wanted to carry her off to bed. But, damn it, that was no reason to let her lead him around by the nose! She was too independent for her own good, stubborn as hell, persistent, determined to have her own way. But he couldn't even begin to contemplate what his life would be like without her.

The door to the master bedroom was pulled open, and suddenly she was there in the hall before him. He scowled, his body jumping to life at the sight of her dressed in a pink print blouse and white summer skirt. How could she possibly be more beautiful than he remembered?

Georgia froze, her hand at her throat as her shocked eyes took in his towel-clad figure. She hadn't expected to see him. "I thought you'd already be gone," she said in a strained voice, retreating from the hostility she saw in his eyes. How many mornings had she lain in their bed and listened to him leave before the sun came up?

"There's plenty of time," he replied curtly.

She hardly heard him. Her eyes were mesmerized

by the angles and planes of his hard body, his broad, powerful shoulders, the rippling, sinewy beauty of his muscles. The clean, spicy scent of him attacked her senses, clouding her mind with memories of their loving, and her only desire at that moment was to touch him. Without conscious thought, her hand lifted to his hair.

He caught her wrist in midair and forced it back down to her side. "Don't," he growled softly.

The blood drained from her face. "You don't want me to touch you?"

"No." When she touched him, he forgot his resolve not to make love to her until he could give her the words she needed to hear, he forgot the dangers of letting her into his heart. "I won't let you tease me until I'm so hungry for you I'll say anything you want."

She laughed sharply, painfully. "Don't worry, Wes, I'm not going to pounce on you. But since I make you so nervous, I'll gladly vacate the premises." Pivoting away from him, she marched into the bedroom and grabbed a small overnight bag from the closet, her movements stiff. "I've taken all the garbage from you I'm going to take," she said coldly as she dumped a few essentials into the bag and snapped it shut. "When you decide to quit acting like a spoiled brat, let me know."

He watched her take a plastic-wrapped evening dress from the closet and pick up the suitcase before he could force his feet to move. He stepped in front of her, blocking her way. "Where the hell do you think you're going?"

Her eyes shot daggers at his tone. "To the boat. In case you've forgotten, we're giving a party tonight.

And unless you intend to lock me in this room, you'd better get out of my way. I've got some things to do for tonight, and I can't afford to waste any more time."

For a minute he looked as if he was going to throttle her, but she looked him squarely in the eye, daring him to touch her. He stepped back. What had he done? He hadn't meant a word of what he'd said; surely she knew that. He'd only needed a little more time to adjust to the fact that he was crazy about her, but he'd pushed her too far. She was leaving him. And he was standing here like an idiot, letting her go. "Georgia . . . honey, wait!"

She shook his hand off her arm. "Don't touch me!" she said in a voice that dripped icicles. "You've said all I want to hear. I'm getting out of here before you make me say something I might regret."

She walked past his stiff figure with her chin held high, but the tears fell when she reached her car. All her hopes were gone, her worst fears realized. Their marriage had been a mistake from the beginning. He wanted a divorce.

12

~~~~~~~~~

She never knew how she made it through the day. She wanted to crawl into a hole somewhere and hide from the world, to pull her broken heart back together and give it time to mend. But she couldn't. There were a thousand-and-one last-minute details that required her attention, a crowd of employees that were looking to her for direction because Wes was nowhere to be found. So she stiffened her backbone and glued on a frozen smile, shutting her mind to the constant, unrelenting pain that wracked her body.

By the time evening approached everything was ready. The old riverboat was breathtaking, its mahogany and oak wood gleaming in the lamplight, its brass sparkling. Fresh flowers adorned every table and the musicians were warming up. The guests would be arriving within the hour.

When Georgia slipped into Wes's stateroom to

change, the pretense of happiness she'd been clinging to all day dropped from her like a cloak. She leaned wearily against the closed door, on the verge of physical and mental exhaustion. She was a fool to punish herself this way. When would she be able to think of Wes without hurting? A year from now? A lifetime?

Never, she admitted sadly. She'd given her heart forever.

Depression weighted her shoulders as she headed for the shower. It seemed to be the fate of the Dupree women to fall for men who couldn't return their love.

When she stepped from the stateroom a short while later, however, there was no sign of that depression. If Wes was going to ease her out of his life, she was going out in style, with a smile on her lips and in her eyes.

Her dress was a dream. Romantic, daring, exceedingly sensuous, it called to mind fairy tales and daydreams, waltzing and Rhett Butler. It was perfect for the opening of the riverboat restaurant. It was also deliciously naughty. At first glance, she appeared to be wearing an off-the-shoulder emerald ball gown that hugged her breasts and small waist before flaring to a full, flounced skirt that whispered with every step she took. But closer scrutiny revealed a tantalizing amount of creamy bare skin, a neckline that teasingly dipped between her breasts, and a bodice that somehow allowed a shocking view of her curves should she be so foolish as to lean over. A sudden vision of Wes accusing her of teasing him popped into her head, and she grinned. She might be tempted to lean over for him.

The night was warm, the lap of the dark water languid against the sides of the boat as she made her way toward the main-deck lounge. Wes would be there by now, waiting to receive their guests, and this would probably be her only chance to catch his reaction to her dress. She couldn't help hoping she'd knock him out of his socks.

But he wasn't there. The room was empty except for the white-coated employees who would circulate among the guests with champagne and hors d'oeuvres.

"Where the hell is he?" she muttered to herself.

"I don't know," a gravelly voice replied. "But once he sees you in that dress, he'll probably lock you in his stateroom."

She spun around, a light blush stealing over her cheeks, and whistled softly at the sight of Pierce decked out in a black tux. "Look at you!" she teased. "Maybe I should lock you up. You're gorgeous!"

"Hmp!" he snorted disapprovingly, but Georgia could tell by the glow in his blue eyes that he was pleased. "I must have been out of my mind to let Wes talk me into wearing this penguin suit. I'm the pilot, for God's sake!"

"The best dressed one on the river," she agreed as she reached up to straighten his black tie, soft laughter spilling into her eyes. "You're also one of his best friends and you can't hide upstairs all evening like a hermit."

"I'm not the one hiding," he reminded her pointedly. "Where's that husband of yours? I haven't seen him all day."

She sobered, her worried gaze drawn to the French doors that offered a view of the gangplank. "I don't know. I haven't seen him either. And here come the first guests. Looks like you're going to have to help me greet them, Pierce. I don't know half the people we invited."

He went with her grudgingly, grumbling all the way. "Wes is going to pay for this," he muttered under his breath. "First the suit and now this. I want a raise! This isn't in my job description. . . ."

"It's not in mine either," she said between her teeth, a strained smile cracking her face, "but somebody's got to do it. And you can't have a raise because I'm going to kill him!"

She had plenty of time to figure out how she was going to do it. Over an hour, in fact. Her father and Kurt arrived, as did Jenny and a hundred people she didn't know, and Wes was still embarrassingly absent. The excuses she made for him soon began to sound hollow even to her own ears, and when she wasn't contemplating his early demise, she was worried sick about him. She was just about to ask Pierce to go look for him when she looked across the room and found herself snared by her husband's dark eyes.

Her heart stumbled, missing a beat, and if she hadn't clutched at Pierce's arm, her legs would have given way beneath her. Her eyes drank in the sight of him, his thick, black hair, his boyish smile, the slim, taut body that looked so comfortable in a tuxedo. She would have run to him if she could have convinced her feet to move.

But he never even made an attempt to approach her. Stunned, she watched him nod coolly before grabbing a glass of champagne from a passing waiter and turning to circulate among the guests. Georgia's temper exploded like an atom bomb.

She was going to boil him in oil!

She started toward him, but came up short as a

strong, masculine arm slipped around her waist. "Don't do it, sis," Kurt laughed in her ear. "You'll only regret it when you cool off."

"I'll regret it if I don't," she snapped, trying without success to push his arm away. "Damn it, Kurt, let go of me! You can't stop me from talking to my husband."

"Oh, really? I thought I had."

"You're asking for it, little brother," she warned, her eyes narrowed dangerously. "I'm not in the mood for this. *Let go!*"

"I will when you promise you're not going to go over there and try to take Wes apart limb by limb."

"Since when have you started taking his side over mine?"

He swore softly. "I'm not taking sides. But in case you've forgotten, there are several reporters here. I know you couldn't care less about that right now, but do you want the whole city to read about a fight between you and Wes in tomorrow's paper?"

"Of course not!" She slumped against him in defeat. "I am not going to let him get away with this, Kurt. When this party is over . . ."

"He'd better run for his life," he replied with a grin.

"You're damn right!"

For the next hour Georgia was careful to always keep a crowd between Wes and herself, and if her smile was a little strained, her laughter slightly forced, no one noticed. Fury added a sparkle to her eyes and gave her the strength to act as if she was having a wonderful time; before too long it wasn't an act. Her anger drained away, and she found herself relaxing, her smile coming more naturally. She had lost sight of Pierce, but Kurt was always close by, there to make her laugh even when she was determined not to, teasing her about the beautiful women Wes had invited. From across the room they watched him talking to Jenny before leading her over to a dark-haired giant to make introductions. Georgia smiled to herself at Jenny's apparent delight with the new man.

"Still think he's like Dad?" her brother asked quietly.

Her eyes silently shifted to her father, who had come to the party alone but was now flirting charmingly with a curvaceous blonde who looked as if she hadn't a thought in her head. "No," she said softly as her gaze swung back to her husband. "I tried to make myself believe that so I wouldn't fall in love with him. It didn't work."

She'd known all along she was only kidding herself. Now that she had quit fighting her heart, she could see that any similarities between Wes and her father were only superficial. Granted, they were both handsome, charming men, but her father was a philanderer, and that was something Wes would never be. Wes had just as many men friends as women, and although he played the charming host to the hilt, he never actually flirted with any of the beautiful, sophisticated women who crossed his path. He seemed immune to their batting lashes and swaying hips.

Just watching him made her breath catch in her throat and her pulses pound. He was easily the handsomest man in the room. With his wicked, laughing eyes and flashing grin, he was rakishly attractive, and she wouldn't have blamed any woman there for throwing herself at him. But she couldn't. He didn't want her to touch him.

Suddenly the press of human bodies was too much, and she had to escape. She turned to her brother, her face pale. "I'm going to slip outside for a while. I need some air."

He frowned, concern clearly written in his eyes. "Want me to come with you? You're not sick, are you?"

"No. I just need some time to myself." She gave him a weak smile. "Quit worrying about me and go find someone to dance with."

He looked as if he might argue, so she hurried away before he had the chance, winding her way through the crowd as quickly as she could. She had almost reached the French doors when she ran into Jenny. She bit back a groan and struggled to find a smile. "I thought you were dancing with Wes's friend."

"Oh, I was," the redhead laughed, her blue eyes sparkling like sapphires. "He's getting us something to drink and then we're going to stroll around the deck. Oh, Georgia, isn't he the most gorgeous hunk you've ever seen in your life! Aside from Wes," she quickly amended. "I know you're crazy about him. Hey, are you all right?" she demanded suddenly, noticing for the first time her friend's pained expression. "Would you like me to find Wes for you?"

"No!" At Jenny's startled expression, she grimaced. "It's just a stupid headache. Don't bother Wes. He's having too much fun."

"Are you sure?" she argued. "You're awfully pale."

"It's just tension. I'll feel better after I get some air," Georgia insisted firmly. "Would you mind filling in for me as hostess for a few minutes? I hate to ask you to give up your walk in the moonlight but . . ."

Jenny pushed her through the double doors before the words were even out of her mouth. "Of course not, silly. What are neighbors for? Go lie down for a while and don't worry about me. The moon's not going anywhere for hours yet."

Georgia couldn't find the strength to argue further and thankfully stepped outside. But at the sight of the couples walking the decks arm in arm, her spirits dropped to her feet. She wasn't the only one who had turned her back on the merriment inside in favor of the gentle quiet of the night. She might as well go back inside, she thought wearily. She'd find no solitude here.

But when she pivoted back toward the lounge, her gaze snagged on the narrow flight of stairs that zigzagged up the side of the boat, and her eyes slowly lifted to the small cabin that sat on the roof of the top deck. The pilothouse. It would be quiet there.

The stairs were steep and poorly lit, and she was breathless when she reached the top. She pulled open the door and almost stepped off the landing in fright when someone moved in the shadowy darkness. "Who's there?" she demanded sharply.

"I am," Pierce growled as he stepped into the light. "But for God's sake, don't tell anyone! This is the only quiet place on the whole boat."

"So this is where you're hiding." She shut the door behind her. "I should have known."

"I couldn't take it anymore," he admitted gruffly. "What brings you up here?"

"The peace and quiet." She wandered over to one of the wide windows and stared out at the night. She could see everything . . . the lovers on the deck below who thought they were unobserved, the ships moored up and down both sides of the river, the French Quarter. She looked over her shoulder and smiled into his eyes. "It's a shame Danny couldn't have been here tonight, but I suppose this is sort of stuffy compared to a RUSH concert." She sighed. "But I could stay up here the rest of the night."

"Wes will be worried about you. Does he know where you are?"

Her eyes snapped back to the view. "No, but he doesn't need me. The waiters will start showing everyone upstairs to the dining room any minute now. I won't be missed."

He opened his mouth to protest, but the phone rang, cutting him off. He reached for it. "Yes?"

"Is Georgia up there?" Wes demanded curtly in his ear.

"Yes."

"Is she all right?"

The older man smiled at the concern in his friend's voice. "Probably."

Wes swore softly. "What the hell is that supposed to mean, Pierce? Either she is or she isn't. Never mind. I'll find out for myself. Send her down to our stateroom."

"Are you sure you want me to do that?" the pilot asked doubtfully. "I don't think that would be a very smart move right now."

"I don't care. I want to talk to her now; and if she's not down here in five minutes, I'm coming up after her."

"Wes—" he protested warningly, but the line went dead and, with a sigh, he hung up. That boy had a lot to learn about women. Especially this woman. He turned and found her eyes upon him.

Uneasiness gripped Georgia, but her voice was steady when she asked, "What did he want?"

He hesitated, but when her eyes narrowed determinedly, he knew he had no choice. "He wants to see you in your stateroom in five minutes. To talk."

A feminine brow arched dangerously. "Oh, really? And who gave him the right to order me around?"

"I guess you did," Pierce said with a grin. "Or Wes seems to think you did."

"Then he's in for a rude awakening," she replied grimly. "I don't jump just because Wesley Hayden snaps his fingers."

The laughter fell from the older man's face. "He threatened to come after you, Georgia. He doesn't make idle threats."

He would do it, too, she thought furiously. He wouldn't think twice about embarrassing her in front of everyone. Damn it, she wouldn't let him do that to her! She marched over to the door and pushed it open angrily. "All right, I'll go. But if he thinks I'm going to let him get away with this, he's crazy!"

The door slammed behind her. Damn him! Who did he think he was? She would not be ordered around like a child. Just because he wanted a divorce, that was no reason— She stopped, her heart slamming against her ribs. Surely he wasn't going to tell her now. He couldn't be that cruel. But he'd practically promised he'd tell her how he felt by tonight, a tiny voice reminded her. And the party was almost half over.

She sank down onto one of the iron steps, unmindful of her dress, her heart assaulted by a terrible, cold emptiness. How could she walk into their stateroom knowing what he was going to say to her? She couldn't just calmly stand there and let him tell her it was over. If he apologized for not loving her, she'd just die.

But wouldn't it be better to get it over with now? her

heart reasoned. While there was a crowd of people around and she wouldn't have to be alone with him? Somehow she would have to be cool, unemotional, detached. He wouldn't want a messy scene, and neither did she. She couldn't let him drag it out. She wouldn't be able to hold back the tears for long.

Wes paced the confines of the stateroom like a condemned man, his emotions torn between anger and fear as five minutes came and went. She wasn't coming, he thought in despair. This morning he'd finally pushed her too far, and now she was showing him it was over. Damn his miserable tongue! He'd fought against needing her, loving her, and never realized that she'd already found a place in his heart. But now it was too late. He'd driven her away.

Rage boiled within him. Her scent, her touch, were everywhere . . . in the wild flowers on the dresser, the red carpet she had insisted upon, the bed he could so easily picture her in. Would he ever be able to walk onto this boat again without listening for her footstep, her laughter?

With a groan, he dropped to the edge of the mattress and buried his face in his hands. How could he have been so stupid as to lose her twice in one lifetime?

He was still sitting that way when Georgia silently stepped into the room. Her breath caught in her throat at the sight of his desolate figure. He looked miserable, his shoulders hunched against a pain that came from within, his dark hair ruffled, as if he'd repeatedly run his hands through it. Her heart twisted in her breast. The need to touch him, console him was all consuming, but his words from that morning rang in her ears and nailed her feet to the floor.

The sudden click of the latch was like a clap of thunder in the quiet room. Wes's head jerked up, his tortured eyes impaling her to the door. He surged to his feet. "Georgia!"

"You wanted to see me?" she said stiffly as she pushed herself away from the door on legs that refused to stop trembling.

His gaze roamed her pale face hungrily. "Jenny told me you weren't feeling too well," he finally said hoarsely. "I just wanted to make sure you were all right."

"What!" she laughed incredulously. "I don't believe this! You *ordered* me down here for that?"

"I was worried about you," he said defensively, irritation tightening his mouth into a thin line. "You disappeared. I didn't know if you'd collapsed somewhere or run off."

"Why would you care one way or the other?"

"Because you're my wife. You carry my name. It's my responsibility to take care of you."

His voice was laced with impatience, but there was something in his eyes that wouldn't let her accept his pat explanation. She stepped toward him, suddenly willing to risk everything for what she had seen in his eyes. "That's not good enough, Wes. Caring for someone isn't a responsibility. You don't do it because you have to. So why do you care, Wes? Tell me. *Please.*"

His wary eyes searched hers, but at the sight of the love she made no attempt to hide, he groaned and snatched her into his arms. "Because I love you," he said in a fierce whisper against her hair. "I love you." His hands came up to tenderly frame her face, pulling her back until his eyes could capture hers. "Do you hear me, honey? I love you, and I was so afraid I'd lost you. This morning—"

Her fingers pressed against his mouth. "Forget this morning," she said softly, a tender smile glowing from the depths of her eyes. "It isn't important."

"I didn't mean it the way you took it," he continued stubbornly, guiding her hand back to his mouth to place a kiss on the sensitive palm before lightly touching his tongue to the inside of her wrist. His body caught fire just watching her eyes darken and smolder. "If I hadn't said those things, we'd have ended up in bed. And I wasn't ready."

"Are you now?" she asked huskily.

"What do you think?" he growled, pressing her hips intimately to his, letting her feel his arousal.

Her breath left her lungs in a rush as desire ran through her body in a delicious shiver. Wicked, wanton thoughts tempted her until she ached to push him onto the bed and drive him wild with her hands and mouth. But how could she when they were in the middle of giving a party? "Wes, the party . . ."

"To hell with the party," he whispered, deliberately rocking his hips against hers. At her gasp, his black eyes reflected the fire that burned in his loins. "Let me love you, honey," he coaxed in a rough voice. "Let me show you what you mean to me. It'll be good. I promise, sweetheart. Don't say no."

She couldn't, not when he rubbed his thumb across her bottom lip until her mouth throbbed for his kiss, not when his words turned her insides to a seething mass of need. She clung to him, resentment flaring briefly in her eyes. "Damn it, Wes, you don't play fair! Everyone's going to be wondering where we are."

"Will you stop worrying?" he chided. "I'll take care

of everything while you get ready for bed." And before she could protest, he turned her around and playfully swatted her on the rear. "Go on," he laughed. "I've got to call Pierce, and you're distracting the hell out of me."

She grinned, her eyes dancing with promises. "You ain't seen nothin' yet!"

"I'll hold you to that," he growled and reached for the phone on the bedside table, his eyes lingering on Georgia as she walked to the opposite side of the bed to turn down the bedspread. When his friend came on the line, he said, "Let's take a run down river, Pierce. Georgia wants to see the city by moonlight again, and tonight she can have anything she wants."

He grinned at her indignant gasp, but his laughter nearly choked him when she braced both hands in the middle of the bed and leaned toward him. "Anything?" she purred.

Wes's eyes were riveted to the bodice of her dress, gaping away from her body to reveal the luscious curves of her breasts. His mouth went dry, the phone forgotten in his hand as he devoured every beautiful inch of her. "Dear God, where did you get that dress?"

"What dress?" Pierce demanded, confused.

"What? Oh, not you, Pierce," he said quickly, frowning fiercely when Georgia giggled. "Tell our guests they're going for a ride down river. And would you ask Jenny to make apologies for Georgia? She has a migraine and I can't leave her."

"She must be out of her head with pain," the pilot replied dryly. "I can hear her laughing. Good night, Wes. And congratulations."

He grinned. "Thanks." When Wes hung up, he

started toward her with a reproving frown that was belied by the twinkle in his eyes. "That's some dress."

She dimpled and twirled before him, her skirt teasingly brushing his legs. "It does have a certain style, doesn't it? I thought you'd like it."

"How many times have you leaned over tonight?"

She bit back a smile, pretending to consider. "Let's see. I had to bend over to put on my hose. And my shoes, of course. . . ."

"Georgia!"

Her eyes laughed at his warning tone as she looped her arms around his neck. "You're acting like a jealous husband," she chided and kissed the corner of his mouth. "There's no reason to be. No one's seen me but you."

He groaned and crushed her to him. "What am I going to do with you?"

"Love me, I hope."

"Always," he growled, then leaned down to capture her parted lips with his.

Silhouette Desire Romances

TAKE 4
THRILLING SILHOUETTE
DESIRE ROMANCES
ABSOLUTELY FREE

Experience all the excitement, passion and pure joy of love. Discover fascinating stories brought to you by Silhouette's top selling authors. At last an opportunity for you to become a regular reader of Silhouette Desire. You can enjoy 6 superb new titles every month from Silhouette Reader Service, with a whole range of special benefits, a free monthly Newsletter packed with recipes, competitions and exclusive book offers. Plus information on the top Silhouette authors, a monthly guide to the stars and extra bargain offers.

An Introductory FREE GIFT for YOU.
Turn over the page for details.

As a special introduction we will send you FOUR
specially selected Silhouette Desire romances
— yours to keep FREE — when you complete
and return this coupon to us.

At the same time, because we believe that you will be so thrilled
with these novels, we will reserve a subscription to Silhouette
Reader Service for you. Every month you will receive 6 of the very
latest novels by leading romantic fiction authors, delivered direct to
your door.

Postage and packing is always completely
free. There is no obligation or commitment —
you can cancel your subscription at any time.

It's so easy. Send no money now. Simply fill in and post
the coupon today to:-

**SILHOUETTE READER SERVICE, FREEPOST,
P.O. Box 236 Croydon, SURREY CR9 9EL**

Please note: READERS IN SOUTH AFRICA to write to:-
Silhouette, Postbag X3010 Randburg 2125 S. Africa

FREE BOOKS CERTIFICATE

**To: Silhouette Reader Service, FREEPOST, PO Box 236,
Croydon, Surrey CR9 9EL**

Please send me, Free and without obligation, four specially selected Silhouette Desire Romances and reserve a
Reader Service Subscription for me. If I decide to subscribe, I shall, from the beginning of the month following my
free parcel of books, receive six books each month for £5.94, post and packing free. If I decide not to subscribe I
shall write to you within 10 days. The free books are mine to keep in any case. I understand that I may cancel my
subscription at any time simply by writing to you. I am over 18 years of age.
Please write in BLOCK CAPITALS.

Name _____

Address _____

_____

_____ Postcode _____

SEND NO MONEY — TAKE NO RISKS

*Remember postcodes speed delivery. Offer applies in U.K. only
and is not valid to present subscribers. Silhouette reserve the right
to exercise discretion in granting membership. If price changes
are necessary you will be notified.
Offer limited to one per household. Offer expires April 30th, 1986.*

EP18SD